8^{250}

The door to Whiskers, Wings, and Wags flew open.

"Vanessa!" Jeff's shout almost covered the chimes. A split second later, Vanessa heard Nathan's low scold, "You're not a Scud missile, Son. Use your indoor voice and your manners."

" 'Kay, Dad. Where is she?"

"I'm down here," Vanessa called. She lifted a hand and waved over the counter.

"Hey, Van," Nathan said, "about ready to go?"

Embarrassed to the core of her being, she looked up at Nathan and shook her head.

"No?".

"I'm um. . .stuck."

CATHY MARIE HAKE is a Southern California native who loves her work as a nurse and Lamaze teacher. She and her husband have a daughter, a son, and two dogs, so life is never dull or quiet. Cathy considers herself a sentimental pack rat, collecting antiques and Hummel figurines. She otherwise keeps busy with reading, writing, baking, and being a prayer warrior. "I am easily distracted during prayer, so I devote certain tasks and chores to specific requests or persons so I can keep faithful in my prayer life."

Books by Cathy Marie Hake

HEARTSONG PRESENTS
HP370—Twin Victories
HP481—Unexpected Delivery
HP512—Precious Burdens

Love Is Patient

Cathy Marie Hake

Heartsong Presents

To those who love and sacrifice and to those who patiently walk alongside and wait. God bless you.

I'd like to thank Rick Wilcox of Guide Puppies for the Blind. He was a wonderful resource. All of the right information about the dogs is his; any mistakes are mine.

A note from the Author:
I love to hear from my readers! You may correspond with me by writing:

> **Cathy Marie Hake**
> **Author Relations**
> **PO Box 719**
> **Uhrichsville, OH 44683**

ISBN 1-58660-806-1

LOVE IS PATIENT

PRINTED IN THE U.S.A.

one

Granite Cliffs, California

Big, brown, puppy-dog eyes—Vanessa Zobel had always been a sucker for them. It was why she'd opened Whiskers, Wings, and Wags. Right now, she had not one, but two sets of large, soulful brown eyes trained on her. "May I help you?"

"Nobody can help me," the little brown-eyed boy across the counter said in a despondent tone.

Vanessa looked to the adult for an explanation. The tall, sable-haired man stared back at her for a moment, then glanced down at his shuffling son.

"We need to return this." The man set a quart-sized Zip-Tite plastic bag on the counter. It tilted toward the edge, so he caught and scooted the bag closer to the register. Blissfully untroubled by the changing current, the goldfish inside continued to swim tiny laps.

The little boy stuck out a grubby finger and rubbed the edge of the clear plastic bag. "I done wrong."

His confession didn't reveal much information, but he'd admitted responsibility for whatever the problem was. Vanessa hummed. "Is that so?"

"I really, really wanted Goldie. I knew he'd stay little and he'd be quiet."

The man rested his callused hand on the boy's shoulder. "Jeff—"

"I know, Dad. I done wrong." The little boy hung his head.

Kids sometimes shoplifted. Vanessa had experience dealing with customers in that realm, but she knew Jeff couldn't have stolen the fish. She looked at the father in puzzlement.

"I understand you give coupons to the school for free goldfish. Jeff forged my signature on the parental permission line."

"Ohh." The picture became clear. She looked from the child to the fish and back again at Jeff. His lower lip protruded in a quivering, almost-ready-to-cry pout. "Oh, my."

"Dad says I gotta—" His little chin rose as he sucked in a gulp of air. "Gotta give Goldie back to you."

Vanessa shot the broad-shouldered father a quick glance. The left side of his mouth kicked up into a rakish smile, and his eyes stayed steady as could be. He stood behind his son and kept a hand on his shoulder.

To Vanessa, it looked like a show of support during a difficult time. Still, the father's other palm flattened and scooted the baggy farther away. Taking her cue from him, she walked around the counter and knelt in front of the little guy. Since she didn't know if he would be afraid of her dog, she rested a hand on Amber's golden coat in a silent show of reassurance. "Jeff, I think you're a mighty lucky young man."

"You mean I getta keep Goldie?" Hope flared in his big eyes.

"No, I'm afraid not." Vanessa took his little hand in hers as she shook her head. "I think you're blessed to have a daddy who loves you so much, he wants to teach you to be an honorable man."

"Is honor'ble like being honest?"

"That's part of it. It means being honest and fair and that folks know they can trust you to do the right thing."

Jeff twisted the toe of his well-worn sneaker on the

linoleum floor. The sound of the rubber squeaking mixed with tweets, yips, and a parrot squawk. He jammed his hands into his pockets and muttered, "My dad's honor'ble."

"I try to be, Son. It's not always easy."

Tears filled Jeff's eyes. "I wanna keep Goldie. Goldie likes me. What if he isn't happy here?"

"I'm sure the lady has lots of goldfish to keep Goldie company."

"Yes, I do. Goldie will need to get used to the water, though."

Though lines of bafflement creased his brow, a devastatingly handsome smile tilted the father's mouth. "Goldie's already a very good swimmer."

"I'll need to let him get used to the water temperature. It might be a bit of a shock to him otherwise, so we'll just slip him—bag and all—into the tank until the temperature equalizes. Then we'll let Goldie out so he can make friends with all of the other fish."

"We will? Do I get to help?"

Oops. Me and my big mouth. She wrinkled her nose and looked up at the father again. "It'll take about fifteen minutes."

Jeff tugged on his father's paint-splattered sweatshirt. "Dad, you said we were going to bring Goldie back if it took all day!"

Vanessa tried to smother her smile. She doubted the father meant he was willing to stick around for a fish reacclimation.

The father chuckled and rumpled Jeff's hair. "We can spare fifteen minutes."

Vanessa took the bag from the counter. "The fish tanks are right back here."

"Can I carry Goldie?" A quick look back into the dad's eyes let Vanessa know it was okay. "Sure." She handed the squishy package down to Jeff's little hands, then shoved up the right sleeve of his lightweight sweatshirt. "We'll even have you put his bag into the tank."

Jeff carried his tiny contraband through the store. Vanessa thought they made quite a procession—the boy and his fish, his father, then she and Amber bringing up the rear. Amber quietly sat at heel while the father clasped his big hands around his son's waist and lifted him. Jeff solemnly lowered the bag into the goldfish tank. Big tears filled his eyes.

"I know it's hard for you, Son, but this is the way it has to be." The father set him back down.

"I knew it was bad to tell a lie. Writing a lie is wrong too, huh?"

"Yes, it is."

Several of the fish in the tank darted by the plastic bag. A few nudged it. "It looks to me like Goldie's got a lot of fish who want to be his friend," Vanessa said. "You can watch them for awhile if you'd like. I need to do a little work around here, but I'll come back to help you let Goldie out of the bag."

Vanessa walked past several more tanks teeming with fish, around the corner display of hamsters, gerbils, and mice, then shoved a protruding bag of dog food into place on a shelf before she reached the back room.

"All done," Valene declared as she pulled a load of towels from the clothes dryer.

Vanessa smiled at her identical twin. "Hang on a second." She unfastened Val's clip, quickly finger combed the shoulder-length, honey blond tresses back into order, and popped them back into a tidy ponytail that matched her own.

Val's blue eyes twinkled. "If you tell me I look pretty, I'm going to accuse you of being vain."

"Your soul is beautiful," Vanessa shot back. "I didn't say a word about the package God put it in."

"Oh, so He gave Mom and Dad a two-for-the-price-of-one deal on us?"

"Spoken like a business major." Vanessa laughed at their silly banter as she plucked a green jacket from amidst the towels and fastened it over Amber's back. "Speaking of deals, what would you think of us putting together a puppy package?"

"Not a bad idea—especially since you filled every last cage and pen last night."

"What do I say?" Vanessa spread her hands wide. "I love dogs. I need to get back out there." She smoothed the golden retriever's jacket, gave the animal an affectionate stroke, and started to push a cart out the door. "Let's go." She murmured the command, and Amber sedately walked alongside her.

"Watcha doin'?" Jeff asked from over by the hamsters.

"I'm going to give all of the animals some fresh drinking water."

"Can I help?"

"You need to ask your daddy."

Jeff's father turned around from admiring a parrot. "I'll let him help. . . ." Glints of gold sparkled in his brown eyes. "If I can too."

Jeff scampered over. "Your dog's wearing clothes now!"

"Yes, she is. She's a special dog. Her name is Amber."

Jeff pursed his lips and squinted at the writing on the green jacket. He pointed at it. "That doesn't say Amber."

His father squatted down beside him. "Why don't you read it, Sport?"

"J-joo-eye-dee." His little features twisted. "Jooeydie? What is that?"

"Sound it out again. Use the other sound for G, and keep the first vowel silent."

Jeff's face puckered. "Teacher says, 'When two vowels go walking, the first one does the talking.'"

"That's usually true, but this word is a rule breaker."

"G-eye-dy. Guide!" Jeff beamed as he ran his forefinger along the white lettering. "Guide pup-py in train-ing!"

"What a smart boy!" Vanessa smiled at how the father beamed from her praise every bit as much as the son.

"Jeff's six. I'm Nathan Adams." Laugh lines around his mouth deepened. "I'm sure he'll be glad to tell you how old I am, what we ate for lunch, and that I occasionally drive too fast."

"Vanessa Zobel," she provided with a quick laugh. "Twenty-four, a taco, and no speeding tickets. . .yet."

"Did Amber eat a taco too?"

"No." She played with Amber's soft ears. "Amber isn't supposed to be a pet. She's going to be a working dog. We want to teach her to do her jobs without getting treats. It makes her happy for me to pat her and tell her she's a good girl."

Nathan hooked his thumbs in the front pockets of his tattered jeans. "So you'll train her and give her away?"

The gentle quality of his voice made Vanessa's heart melt. Most people focused on what a wonderful thing it was for the blind to receive such a dog. She did too—or she wouldn't be training the dogs. Still, few ever understood the ache involved in relinquishing a puppy.

"This is my fourth guide puppy." She petted Amber and added, "She's a good dog. I'll miss her, but I know she'll be a wonderful companion helper for someone who needs her."

"Does she sleep here at night with all of the other animals?" Jeff continued to trace the letters on the jacket.

"No, Amber goes everywhere with me. It's my job to make sure she learns how to behave nicely wherever we are. In a few months, she'll go to San Francisco to a special doggy school where they'll teach her how to help a blind person."

"Someone's going to be lucky," Nathan said slowly as he

looked into her eyes. "It looks like you've trained Amber magnificently."

"Does she wear that thing on her face 'cuz she's a working dog?"

"Yes." Vanessa glanced down at the green halterlike device. "It's a training tool called a gentle leader. That part around her muzzle is loose, so she can still open her mouth."

"Can she still eat?"

"Yes, she could, but I've trained her only to eat at special times from a bowl. She won't eat food she finds on the ground or that people offer her. See how the other part of it goes under her chin here and makes a collar? If I give the leash just a tiny pull, it steers her."

Nathan gave her an astonished look. "Power steering for puppies. Wow."

"How come all of the other dogs and cats are noisy, but Amber is quiet?"

"They're just babies. They need someone to love and train them." The door chimed. Vanessa craned her neck and spied one of her regular customers trundling into the shop. "Excuse me. I need to help Mrs. Rosetti."

She sold the usual pound of lamb-and-rice biscuits her regular bought each week, then came back to the father and son. "Would you like to help me give the animals fresh water to drink?"

In no time at all Nathan, Jeff, and Vanessa had refilled all the water bottles and dishes for the reptiles, rodents, birds, and kittens. Jeff's enthusiasm for the task far outstripped his ability, and his shirt showed it. Still, his father ignored the wet clothing and patiently helped his son. At each cage, habitat, or pen, Jeff decided he'd love to have that particular pet the most.

"Looks like you have a bona fide animal lover on your hands," she said to Nathan.

"He's decided anything worth having is worth collecting. We already have a rock collection, at least two hundred baseball cards, three oatmeal canisters of seashells, and enough Matchbox cars to jam our own freeway. If I let him have one pet, I'm sure our whole house would turn into one big menagerie."

As Vanessa raised a brow, she asked the teasing question, "And the problem with that would be. . . ?"

"I'm not about to debate that issue with you." Nathan shook his head and gave her a rueful grin. "Your bias is clear."

"True. I think pets are great." Vanessa parked the cart in the corner and spread her hands wide. "I can't think of anything better than being around animals!"

"Why are you stopping?" Nathan asked her.

"We can go release Goldie now."

Jeff stood on tiptoe and peeped over the edge of a pen holding a pair of cocker spaniels. "I wanna see the puppies. They're so little!"

"I tell you what: We'll use up the rest of the water in the pitcher. Then, we can let the goldfish free. Afterward, I'll take care of the rest of the dogs."

Nathan snagged one of a pair of cocker spaniels that bounded out of their pen when Vanessa opened the sliding door. She hastily grabbed the other and laughed as it licked her cheek. "You're gonna run me ragged, aren't you, Frack?"

"Frack?" Father and son asked in unison.

"Frack." She held up her wiggling puppy. "You snagged Frick—for which I'm eternally grateful."

"I wanna hold a puppy too."

"I don't mind your holding a puppy, but perhaps we could find one that's a little less active." Vanessa playfully tousled Frack's ears, then set him back in his pen.

The shop's bell chimed again, announcing another customer.

"If you don't mind, I can help Jeff release the goldfish while you take care of those folks," Nathan offered.

"Fine. Thanks."

Lord, she prayed as she walked off, *see that guy? Gorgeous brown eyes, fabulous sense of honor and ethics, even a dollop of humor. You can find me one of those whenever You're ready.*

Two little girls stood with their mother at the door. "We've come to look at kittens."

"I hope all of the good ones aren't taken!" one girl said.

"I hope not too." Vanessa smiled at them, *but I'm not talking about kittens.*

two

Nathan watched the perky woman and her retriever head for the front of the shop. Her blond ponytail bounced as she walked. It had been a long time since he reacted to such a natural beauty. The moment they made eye contact, his brain went into a free fall, and he'd probably made a total fool of himself gawking at her. She hadn't laughed at how he fumbled and almost dropped that dumb goldfish—a fact for which he was grateful.

Most of all, he appreciated how she'd taken her cues from him and supported how he wanted to discipline Jeff. She hadn't made a big, hairy deal out of the matter, but the way she stood firm about putting Goldie back in the tank reinforced his parental decision. Still, the compassionate way she allowed Jeff to make sure Goldie had new friends would undoubtedly keep him from doing a total meltdown when they left.

"Dad, do you think Goldie will be okay?"

"The lady here is nice, Sport. I think she'll do a great job keeping Goldie happy."

"Prob'ly." Jeff sighed. "I guess we can let him out of his bag now."

Jeff took his sweet time telling Goldie a half dozen "important" things. He then spoke to the rest of the tank's occupants, earnestly telling them all about their wonderful companion as if he'd owned the silly creature for months instead of overnight. Lower lips quivering, Jeff finally freed the fish.

Nathan watched tears fill his son's eyes. He quietly took the soggy bag from Jeff's hands and wished again he hadn't needed to do this. As kids went, Jeff was a great, but Nathan wanted him to grow up to have integrity. Rewarding his dishonesty by letting him keep the fish would be a mistake.

"I can't tell which one is Goldie." Jeff trembled. "Can you?"

Oh, it would be so easy to lie.

"No, Son, but I figure that's a good thing. It means Goldie fits right in and everybody is already playing with him."

"How are you doing, Big Guy?" Vanessa asked softly as she rounded the corner. Nathan watched as she knelt, opened her arms, and Jeff ran to her. She hugged him. "It's not easy to say good-bye, is it?"

Jeff shook his head and burrowed closer to her.

"I'll bet you'd rather grow up to be a good man like your daddy than to keep one little old goldfish."

"Yeah," he agreed, his voice muted against her shoulder. "I done wrong, but Dad said this would make it right."

"The next time you have to choose how to act, I'll bet you do a better job," Nathan said as he slipped his hands around Jeff's waist and lifted him high.

"We can't go yet, Dad. She promised I could hold a puppy."

"I need to get more water. Why don't you two go look at the dogs and decide which one Jeff wants to hold?"

Whiskers, Wings, and Wags certainly boasted a bumper crop of animals. Nathan and Jeff sauntered along the puppy wall. Every breed from Afghans to wiener dogs snuffled, yipped, and wagged from the bright clean pens and cages. A pair of puff-ball-sized huskies tussled over a toy, and a little shar-pei that looked like a rumpled tan sock napped in a corner.

"Does she got any spotty dogs like on the movie?"

"Does she have any spotty Dalmatians?" He tried to correct Jeff's grammar when they were alone. If other folks were around, Nathan preferred to ignore the usual childish mistakes. Evie had loved fine literature, and she would have wanted their son to be well spoken.

"Yeah, Dad. Dalmatians. I forgot that name."

Nathan scanned the pens. "Hmm. No, I don't see any."

"I don't carry them," Vanessa said as she approached. Amber walked at her side, yet a frisky black Lab strained every last inch of the leash Vanessa held in her other hand. "Dalmatians are charming to look at, but they tend to be very high-strung so the pound ends up with lots of them. I'd rather let somebody rescue one than support someone to breed more litters."

Nathan listened to every word she said, but he was even more aware of Jeff's reaction. His son reached up, clutched his hand with a near-death grip and quivered with sheer excitement.

"Is that one for me?"

"Sure," Vanessa said. "Maybe we could let you go into a meeting enclosure so he'll stay corralled."

Jeff rocketed into the three-foot tall enclosure, and the Lab galloped right after him. Vanessa laughingly controlled him until Nathan closed the gate. It wobbled, and he inspected it. "You've got a loose screw."

"Plenty of folks have told me I have a screw loose. No one ever told me I have a loose screw."

Jeff still clutched the leash for dear life. "My dad's in the 'struction business. He knows all 'bout screws an' lumber and stuff."

"You've got a handy dad."

"Uh-huh. Honor'ble too. I wanna grow up to be like him someday."

"Good for you. Those are fine qualities."

The minute Vanessa unhooked the leash, the Lab and Jeff tumbled into a tangle of legs and noise.

"Looks like they're getting along okay," she said after a minute. "I'll let them goof off while I give the rest of these babies a drink."

"Let me help," Nathan offered.

She held up her hand. "I'd rather you stay with Jeff. The puppy is already settling down, but I don't like to leave kids alone with unfamiliar dogs."

"Makes sense. Tell you what. Find a Phillips screwdriver, and I'll fix the hinge for you." Nathan grinned at how the Lab licked the hip of Jeff's jeans. "Do you have food in your pocket?"

"Beef jerky," Jeff confessed. "I wanted a snack while you got your hair cut. He's really smart to find it so fast, isn't he, Dad?"

"Yes, he is."

"Can he have some jerky?"

"No," Vanessa called over. "I have a jar of puppy biscuits on the ledge there. You may give him one of those."

The minute the puppy heard the rattle from the jar, he skidded over and sat on Nathan's foot. *Cute little thing. Hardly longer than my shoe.* "Hungry, Boy?"

A yip served as an answer.

Vanessa went up front to help a few more customers. When she came back, she leaned over the wall and chuckled. Nathan didn't feel self-conscious in the least to have Jeff and the puppy both in his lap. As a matter of fact, he was enjoying every minute of it. He'd be hard pressed to say which one of them wiggled more.

"I try to give each of the puppies a temporary name. The owners are free to change it, but it lets me love them a bit more while they're here. Do you guys have any suggestions for him?"

"Blackie?"

Nathan ruffled Jeff's hair. "That's not a bad suggestion, Sport, but lots of dogs get named that. Why not think of things that are black?"

"Wheels. Tires. Licorice."

"Licorice!" Vanessa clapped. "I like that!"

"Lick for a nickname," Nathan added as the puppy laved his son's face.

Truthfully, Jeff and Lick were getting along famously, which surprised Nathan. Jeff had never shown much interest in animals, but he seemed to be enjoying this little jaunt to the pet store. *I didn't even realize he wanted that dumb fish, either. Maybe I should take him to the zoo. . . .*

"I'll make a little name tag for Lick's pen. He just came in last night."

"You've got a bumper crop of puppies." Nathan tilted his head toward the far wall.

"Spring." She smiled. "The early litters are here, and I just took in several new puppies last night. I'd rather sell puppies and kittens for Easter than bunnies."

"I like dogs better than bunnies," Jeff declared. He stroked Licorice and giggled as the puppy licked him avidly in response.

Nathan focused more attention on Vanessa than his son since Jeff seemed content to play with the puppy. "What's wrong with rabbits?"

"Nothing." She shrugged. "Some folks do beautifully with them, but others don't realize the cute little bunny won't stay tiny and that he likes to eat plants."

"Dad, look. He's so neat!"

Nathan glanced down. "Yeah, he is." He looked back at Vanessa. "Sounds like you're more interested in making good matches than in making a buck."

She flushed with obvious pleasure. "I try."

"Can I give him another biscuit?"

"Sure," Nathan answered absently. The jar rattled. "I'll bet the dog treat manufacturers make a bundle off of you, Vanessa."

A wisp of hair came loose from her ponytail as she shook her head. She tucked the sunny strand back into the clip. "I like to use affection instead of treats."

"Dad, he's got lots and lots of little teeth."

"Yeah, he does." He couldn't recall the last time he'd been around anyone so cheerful. "Working here really suits you."

"It's a blessing to have a job I love."

"You found a screwdriver?"

"Yes—if you really don't mind. . ."

"Not at all."

Nathan shifted into a more comfortable position and continued to carry on some small talk with Vanessa as he fixed the hinge. Jeff broke in with little observations and nonsense, but since he and Licorice kept each other entertained, Nathan continued to focus on Vanessa. Jeff got more insistent, and Nathan put both hands on his son's shoulders to transmit that he needed to settle down and hush a bit.

"I'm gonna get it, aren't I?"

At the same time Jeff spoke, Vanessa asked, "Are you guys about done in there?"

"Yes."

"Wow, Dad. Thanks!"

"Huh?" Nathan gave his son a quick look. His little face radiated with joy.

"I'll take really good care of him. I promise!"

"What?" Nathan cast a baffled glance at Vanessa. She gave him a troubled look.

"He asked if he could have the puppy," she whispered, "and you said yes."

three

Oh, great. The one time I don't give my kid undivided attention, I tell him he can have a dog? I didn't mean that he would get the dog; I meant if he kept interrupting he was going to be in trouble! Nathan took a deep breath and turned back to crush Jeff's hopes.

"Jeff," Vanessa said as she entered the pen. She knelt and made direct eye contact with him. "This is all my fault. Your daddy was answering my question. He wasn't telling you that you could have the puppy."

Jeff wrapped his arms around the puppy's neck, hugged it close, and shook his head. His voice went adamant. "My dad is honor'ble. He said I could have my dog."

"Your daddy is an honorable man, but this was just a misunderstanding. A mistake," Vanessa tried again.

Nathan took a deep breath. "It's a fine puppy."

"See? My dad doesn't lie!"

Vanessa let out a soundless sigh.

"Why don't you let us talk about this for a few minutes?" Nathan asked her.

She stood, clasped her hands at her waist, and tilted her head toward the puppy. "The three of you, or the two of you?"

"Three," Jeff answered promptly. From the way he held onto the little Lab, she suspected a six-point earthquake wouldn't shake them apart.

Vanessa didn't say another word. After she let herself out of the enclosure, Nathan noticed she walked away without that cute bounce she'd had earlier.

Several minutes later, she returned. She seemed subdued.

Instead of wearing that dazzling smile, she avoided making eye contact.

"Hey," he called softly. "We're going to take him. A boy needs a dog."

"Labs make good pets," she said as her face brightened a bit, but it still missed that sparkle he'd noticed earlier. "They do well with children."

"I guess I'd better buy some kibble." Nathan let himself out of the enclosure. "Jeff, you and Lick play for a few more minutes."

"Okay, Dad."

Ten minutes later, Nathan dumped the contents of a red plastic shopping basket onto the counter and shook his head. Two chew toys, a bottle of puppy shampoo, a leash, collar, food and water bowls, all accused him of being a pushover. The large sheepskin bed and the forty-pound bag of puppy kibble leaning against the counter proved he'd done a royal job of painting himself into a very expensive commitment.

Me and my big mouth. I try to teach my son to show integrity and end up buying half of a pet store!

Vanessa caught a jingly ball that started to roll off the counter. From the minute she'd whispered that he'd accidentally agreed to get the dog, she'd changed. She couldn't seem to meet his eyes.

From their conversation, Nathan knew making a good match was important to her. He strove to find a way to reassure her. "Do you have a good vet you recommend?"

"We have a terrific vet who comes here one Saturday a month to give vaccinations, Dr. Bainbridge. If you buy the puppy shot package, it saves you all of the office visit charges."

"Good idea."

She leaned down and pulled out a few leaflets from beneath the counter. As she tucked them into a bag, she said,

"I'm giving you the information on that package, as well as one of the vet's business cards."

"Thanks. I appreciate it."

She continued to avoid looking at him. "I'm also giving you a pet ID tag order form. Fill it out, and we'll order the tags. They're complimentary."

He reached over and captured her hand as she reached for one of the toys. "You don't need to throw in anything. Seriously, this was my choice."

"Hey, Dad!"

"Just a minute, Sport."

Vanessa flashed him a strained smile and pulled away from his touch. "We've been putting together a new puppy package. The first bag of food, a toy, and the tags are included at no charge."

The nape of his neck started to prickle. Nathan wheeled around and stared at Vanessa as she quietly walked up to him and asked, "Are you sure you want to do this? I'll come up with some way to explain it to Jeff."

"There are two of you. Twins." He cast a quick look over his shoulder, then concentrated back on Vanessa. Even though her eyes radiated concern, that little spark was still there—both in her eyes and somewhere deep inside of him. He'd missed that with the other gal.

"We're identical. I'm sorry if you were confused. I didn't realize Valene had come out and started helping you."

He glanced down at Amber. "I should have guessed something was wrong. I didn't see your companion."

"Daa-aad. Look out. There are two—" Jeff galloped around the corner and skidded to a stop. Licorice didn't halt. He charged ahead.

"Whoa!" Vanessa dove for the little puppy.

Nathan got to him first. Licorice sniffed his neck and let

out a happy sounding yap. Vanessa knelt right next to them. Nathan dipped his chin to keep the puppy from licking the ticklish spot beneath his left ear. "I don't want to hear another word about not taking this little fellow home. It's obvious he's chosen us."

*

"Vanessa!" Nathan called as he hastened toward the young woman locking the pet shop door.

She cast a quick glance over her shoulder and grinned. "Hi. How are things going?"

"Not good. We need to talk." Nathan raked his fingers through his hair in a single, impatient swipe. "I'm going insane."

"And you think I have the directions to get there?" She finished locking the shop. "Why does everyone think I'm the crazy sister? No, wait. Don't answer that."

He eyed her white-and-orange baseball uniform with dismay. "Cleats?"

"They're a lot more comfortable than heels. My church team is playing across the street tonight."

A sick feeling churned in his stomach. "And you play."

Her smile gleamed. "Believe me, if I didn't, nobody would ever wrangle me into wearing this uniform. I look more like the Great Pumpkin than the shortstop."

He tilted his head to the side. "Shortstop, huh. No kidding? I would have pegged a bouncy gal like you to be the team mascot."

"That was back in high school. Valene was the class valedictorian; I was the class clown and mascot. I shouldn't complain about this uniform. Nothing could ever be as uncomfortable as the shark suit I wore."

"You wore an outfit made of sharkskin?"

"Worse," she moaned. "I wore a great big, gray-and-white plush—"

"Plush? A shark?"

"Oh, yes. Fins and all. You're looking at one of Granite Cliffs's great whites—retired, of course."

"Since you've retired, you'll have enough time to help me." Nathan felt a small spurt of satisfaction that he'd segued this smoothly. "We're um. . .having some trouble."

"We are?" She pointed across the street to the ball diamond in a silent invitation to walk along with her.

Nathan automatically stood to her left so he'd be on the outside. "Yeah, well—"

She didn't follow along. "I'm sorry, Nathan, but Amber walks at heel. You need to be on my right."

"Oh. Okay." He shifted.

"Let's go," she said, and they fell into step.

"See? That's what I need. Jeff and Lick are romping everywhere and tearing up the house and yard. I need obedience and control tips. Amber heard you and fell right into step with us."

"One down, one to go." She winked and added, "I think you do fine with Jeff. The puppy might take a bit of time."

"If you saw my place, you wouldn't say so. My son's decided wherever he goes, Lick should be there with him. Last night, he waited until my back was turned and decided Lick belonged in the tub with him."

"Oh, no!"

Nathan rubbed his forehead at the memory of the wet puppy, the soggy bathroom, and the water trail down the hallway. That was just a part of the trials he faced with this new acquisition. "Yes. The dog won't eat his kibble. Instead, he's chewed the leg of a dining chair and gnawed on a pillow from the sofa."

They stopped at the corner and prepared to cross the busy intersection. Amber halted and sat without any cue at all. A cat streaked by, but the dog didn't react.

"I can't believe that. I've chased after our puppy twice because he can't leave cats alone. You've got to help me."

"I guess I sort of got you into this." Vanessa started to cross the street.

"Are you going to get me out of it?" He matched her stride and added on in desperation, "I'm more than willing to pay the going rate."

"Licorice is too young yet for training, but we can reserve a spot for him in one of the classes I'll have in a little over a month."

"My sanity could be measured in milliseconds, not months."

"Uh-oh. That sounds serious."

He rubbed his aching temple with his fingertips. "The only pets I ever had were cats. Cats take care of themselves."

"Ah, yes. Cats train their owners; dogs are trained by their owners."

"You nailed it on the head. So tell me: What's available right now to get us through the nightmare stage?"

"You mean something like private puppy lessons?"

He shot her a grateful smile. "I thought you'd never offer!"

Her eyes widened and a hectic flush filled her cheeks. "I didn't!" He continued to stare at her, and she scrunched her nose. "Let me guess. You bought the Lab because you misspoke and honored your word, so you're standing there thinking I ought to do the same thing."

"I'm flexible with hours."

Vanessa leaned her back into the fence. One of her knees crooked outward and her heel fit into the chain link. "We have to have an understanding. I'm not good at minding what I say. Valene—she's one of those 'think first, then talk' kind of people. Me? I'm impulsive. She got the brain, and I got the mouth." She laughed self-consciously. "If I'm willing to work with you, you have to promise not to use my words against me. I'll be sunk if you do!"

"Fair enough. When can we start?"

She shrugged. "Tomorrow at seven?"

"A.M.?"

Vanessa groaned. "Oh, don't tell me you're one of those morning people!"

"No." He watched someone dump several bats and balls out of a canvas sack. "I'd be a night owl if Jeff weren't such an early riser. He got that from my wife."

"If she's a stay-home mom, I could work with her from ten to eleven."

Pain speared through him. "Evie died five years ago."

"I'm so sorry, Nathan."

He nodded his head in acknowledgment of her sympathy.

"Nate? Nate Adams!" Kip Gaterie jogged over and shook his hand. "Did Van talk you into joining the team? We could use a slugger like you!"

"Do you play?" Vanessa gave him an assessing and hopeful look.

"Hang on a second here. I'm trying to get you to train a dog so I won't have to chase after him. Running after a ball isn't any more appealing."

"Pity." Kit looked at him steadily. "You can always change your mind. We'd be glad to have you, and we've got a bunch of rug rats about Jeff's age who could keep him company on the playground."

"Thanks, but I'll have to pass."

"That's a shame." Kip scuffed his foot in the red dirt. "Van, the park messed up on our reservation and only slotted us for an hour and a half. We're playing sudden death tonight, so we need to get out there."

"Okay."

As she turned to go, Nathan grabbed her arm. "Hey, if

you're only going to play for a little while, I can go home and get Jeff and Lick. Could you work with us after the game?"

"You're really desperate, aren't you?"

"In a word, yes!"

She glanced at her bright yellow Tweety Bird watch. "Be here at seven-thirty. I can't work miracles, but I'll try to give you a few starting tips."

"I gave up hoping for miracles years ago." He fished in his pocket for his keys, embarrassed by his sharp tone. "Have a good game. We'll be back later."

four

Vanessa wondered at the depth of the bitterness in Nathan's words, but it was neither the time nor the place to ask him what had caused that shift in him. Instead, she shoved on her mitt and jogged out onto the ball diamond.

After a cursory warm-up, the game began. Valene arrived and sat in the bleachers. She liked individual sports like tennis and badminton, but when it came to team sports, she preferred to be a spectator. By contrast, Vanessa loved all sports. She'd begged and wheedled to have her twin join several teams with her, but their youth pastor once gave a lesson on accepting loved ones instead of trying to change them. His words hit home—Vanessa had spent the whole ride to Seaside Chapel trying to cajole Val into trying out for the junior high volleyball team. She spent the drive home apologizing. Now it all seemed to work out beautifully. Val always brought the team banner and would watch Amber while Van dashed around the bases.

Kip sat down on the bench next to Van in the dugout. He nudged her shoulder playfully. "What's with you and Nathan Adams?"

Vanessa gave him a startled look. "Nothing. I just sold him a puppy, and it needs a bit of training. Why?"

He shrugged. "He's a good guy."

She gave him a piercing look. His tone a message she couldn't quite interpret. "But?"

"Nate took his wife's death hard. They used to attend Mercy Springs with me. He stopped attending, and I kinda hoped maybe he was starting back into fellowship."

"I don't know a thing about where he stands with the Lord. The only thing I know is, I'm in the doghouse 'cuz he bought a rambunctious puppy from me." She squinted as a ball sailed through the air. Hopping to her feet, she screamed, "Run! Run, Todd!"

The team cheered as Todd sped across home plate. Kip headed out of the dugout and hefted a bat. He looked back at Vanessa and wagged the end of the bat in her direction. "You never know what God will use to bring a sheep back into the fold. Keep your heart and eyes open."

❧

"There she is!" Jeff galloped toward the chain-link fence. Lick romped alongside him.

Nathan didn't need his son to point out where Vanessa was. He heard her first. She ran full tilt for third base, screaming like a heat-seeking missile the whole way. Her golden ponytail streamed behind her, and the left half of what had once been white-and-orange-striped baseball leggings now sported a calf-to-waist dusting of red that tattled on what must've been a world-class slide. She took a cue from the third-base coach and stopped. Energy high, she bobbed up and down on the base.

Nathan grinned as he continued to watch her. She cheered from third base, "You can do it, Della! Slug it!"

"I don't have your muscles, Girlfriend!"

Cupping her hands around her mouth, Vanessa yelled back, "Then use your brains. Anyone has more of those than I do!"

Everyone on the diamond chuckled, but Nathan watched as the outfielders drew closer to the infield. The ball whizzed over the plate.

"Strike one!" The second pitch went wide. The third zoomed over the plate again. Della stood there the whole time and didn't swing at all.

"Della," Vanessa hollered, "I said to use your brains, not your looks."

Della lifted the bat off her shoulder and took an awkward stance. "I'm not getting filthy dirty like you do."

"Don't worry about that. I already collected all of the loose dirt. You ought to be fine."

"Do you girls mind if we play ball?" the opposing pitcher asked in a humored tone.

"If you insist." Della nodded. "I'm as ready as I'm gonna get."

Nathan's jaw dropped as he heard the bat crack and the ball sailed far out into center field. Vanessa and the runner on second base both ran home. Vanessa skipped back and forth along the foul line. "You did it, Della! You did it!"

"Pretty clever strategy," Nathan said through the fence to Kip. "Lulled the other team into complacency."

Kip shook his head. "Nope. We can't believe it, either. Della's never even connected. Van took her to the batting cages this week."

"What in the world is Della doing on a team if she can't hit?"

"It's not about winning—it's about having a good time." Kip stared at him. "Though I wasn't kidding that we could sure use you on our team."

Vanessa bounced over. "Jeff! Lick! Hiya, guys!"

Licorice jumped up onto the fence with a happy yip.

"Off." Vanessa's voice took on a firm quality. She added, "Give the command and jerk back on the leash."

"Off!" Nathan pulled the leash from Jeff and tugged it. To his surprise, Licorice got all four paws on the grass and gave him a baffled look.

"Good dog, good dog," Vanessa crooned. She glanced at her watch. "You're a little early. Val and Amber are over on the bleachers. You can join them, or I can meet you by the playground as soon as the game is done."

"No playground," Jeff said morosely. "Dad said I can't 'cuz I already took my bath."

"Maybe next time," Vanessa said.

Nathan watched his son brighten up again. Vanessa had a knack for saying the right thing. Licorice started to drag on the leash. "I guess we're off to the stands."

He greeted Valene and took a seat next to her. He leaned forward and read the scoreboard. "The Altar Egos?"

"Vanessa named the team when it got started. She came up with over a dozen possible names, but that one won the vote."

"Is she always this irrepressible?"

Valene choked back a laugh. "I don't think I've ever heard anyone label her that way, but you're right."

The teams swapped positions. Vanessa played shortstop.

"Altar egos. . . ," Nathan repeated as he spotted the big plastic banner someone had tied to the chain-link dugout. The bold black words on the orange-and-white-striped background intrigued Nathan: 'But may it never be that I would boast, except in the cross of our Lord Jesus Christ.' Galatians 6:14.

Kip said it was a game for fun—not for competition—but the banner's declaration backed up what might easily have been a politically correct comment.

Nathan watched as the Altar Ego's players teased each other as much as they congratulated the other team on good plays. Vanessa called, "Nice try!" to one of her teammates when he dropped a pop fly. He picked up the ball, fired it at her, and she snagged it in her glove. "Ned and his nuclear arm!"

She intrigued Nathan. If anyone had room to boast, surely it was Vanessa. A powerhouse hit and a talent for snagging line drives made her impressive to watch. Then again, so did her svelte figure. She'd been almost comical—a one woman cheering squad for her friends. When the clock ran out and her team lost by one run, her grin didn't fade a speck.

As she came over to the bleachers, Jeff hopped up. "Guess what?" He didn't even pause to allow her to guess. "I got new spelling words on Monday, and you'll never in a million years guess what one of the words was. Guide—just like on Amber's jacket."

"Betcha you ace that test," Vanessa said. "Val, we're going to work a little with Licorice to see if we can find a few ways to calm him a bit. You can stay if you'd like, or you can take my car home. Amber and I could use the walk."

"I'd rather go work on my résumé. I saw a few positions in the career section that looked promising." Val squinted at the distance. "I have enough light to walk home. You keep the car."

"Not a chance," Nathan interrupted. "Jeff and I will give Vanessa a ride. We're messing up your schedule. It's the least we can do."

"Really, I can walk," Valene insisted. "I walk or jog four miles every day."

Nathan saw the worried look she shot Vanessa.

"We won't stay very long, Valene. Jeff has school tomorrow, and I need to have him in bed by eight-thirty. After chasing him and Lick around this evening, I'll probably crash all of five minutes later."

"See? Pumpkin time isn't midnight; it's eight." Vanessa handed the keys to her sister. "Now promise me you'll juice up your résumé. It was too modest and bland."

"I'll see what I can do."

"What kind of job are you looking for?"

Valene shrugged. "I have my business degree. I kind of thought maybe a hospital business office."

"The minute you interview, you'll have every single hospital in Southern California after you," Vanessa declared. She stooped and said to Jeff, "My sister is a total brain. She's terrific at spelling words and math."

"Did you ever switch places for tests?" Jeff asked in a stage whisper.

Nathan wondered the same thing, but he wasn't sure he wanted to hear the answer—and he certainly didn't want Jeff to.

Vanessa wrinkled her nose. "It wouldn't have been right for us to swap places at school. We each got the grades we deserved. We did trade places at summer camp once so I could play baseball more and Valene got to swim."

"Van slid into second base and ruined my new jeans that day," Valene recalled.

"You look alike, but you're really different," Jeff decided.

Vanessa winked at Nathan. "That's one smart kid you have there. If your dog is half as clever, training him will be a piece of cake."

They spent about half an hour working with Licorice. Jeff started out like gangbusters, wanting to do everything. Licorice decided to yank free and make a mad dash across the park.

"Oh, no," Nathan groaned. He started to run after the puppy. It was the last thing he wanted to do.

"Nathan, clap and shout his name, but run the opposite way. He'll come chase you."

Less than a minute later, Licorice wiggled in Nathan's arms. "I can't believe it. That's all it takes? I've practically run a marathon twice today, catching this hairy little beast!"

Jeff plopped down on the grass and started to laugh. "Daddy needs to be trained more than the dog!"

Vanessa bit her lip and turned away, but from the way her shoulders shook, he knew she was thoroughly entertained. He bumped her hip with his and said in mock outrage, "Now look what you've done!"

"Saved you shoe leather?" she shot back.

"Who are you kidding?" He held up Licorice. "Knowing my luck, this little energetic four-legged headache is going to end up chewing on my shoes, anyway."

"Dad?"

Something in Jeff's tone made Nathan freeze. "What?"

Jeff ducked his head and lifted both shoulders. He said to his lap in a small voice, "He already did."

Nathan groaned. He turned back to Vanessa. "Shoes, a pillow, and a chair leg. Tell me the list of casualties ends there."

"You're in it for the long haul. It's not a three-strikes-and-he's-out proposition."

"You're the puppy pro." He couldn't help responding to her gentle humor and common sense. "Now what do I do?"

"Give him the chew toys. I don't have anything scheduled tomorrow evening. Bring him by the shop after closing, and we'll come up with some strategies."

"Okay. You're on. I can hold out that long."

❧

The door to Whiskers, Wings, and Wags flew open. "Vanessa!" Jeff's shout almost covered the chimes. A split second later, Vanessa heard Nathan's low scold, "You're not a Scud missile, Son. Use your indoor voice and your manners."

" 'Kay, Dad. Where is she?"

"I'm down here," Vanessa called. She lifted a hand and waved over the counter.

"Hey, Van," Nathan said, "about ready to go?"

Embarrassed to the core of her being, she looked up at Nathan and shook her head.

"No?"

"I'm um. . .stuck."

five

"Stuck?" Nathan repeated, leaning farther over the counter to get a better look.

"Stuck? Vanessa's stuck?" Jeff repeated. He raced around the counter.

"Oh, brother." Vanessa rested her head against Amber's side. "Ever hear the old saying, 'Be careful what you pray for?'"

"What did you pray for, and why are you stuck?" Nathan moved Jeff off to the side and hunkered down.

"I dropped a receipt. It slipped down here behind the drawers. When I reached up to get it, my ring caught, and my hand is jammed."

Nathan thoughtfully pinched his lower lip between his forefinger and thumb. He raised his brows at Jeff. "Son, it looks like we have a genuine damsel in distress here."

"Are we gonna rescue her?"

"Sometimes, Sport, a man's gotta do what a man's gotta do."

"Wait!"

"Did we scare you free, like Dad scares the hiccups outta me?"

"Don't I just wish." She looked up at Nathan. "Would you please flip over the Closed sign and lock the door?"

"Jeff, you heard her. You can do those things, can't you?"

"'Course I can!" His tennis shoes squeaked on the linoleum as he ran back around the counter. The dead bolt made a solid clunk, and cardboard scraped across the glass as the sign flipped over.

Nathan didn't wait for his son to finish those simple tasks.

He slithered onto the floor next to her and slid his hand up close to hers. With each inhalation he took, his chest pressed against her back. Every breath he let out ruffled her hair and made her shiver. He frowned and wrapped his other arm around her. "You're cold. How long have you been trapped down here?"

"Half of forever," she evaded.

"Oh. So she can't tell time, either," Jeff said from behind them.

"Son, we need to squirt some soap up onto Vanessa's hand. Go into the back room and see what you can find."

"Dog shampoo," she suggested. "It's the yellowish orange stuff by the big tub."

Nathan's fingers nudged the side of her hand. "Too bad we can't open the drawer, but it would knock you senseless."

"Thank you."

"Huh?" He twisted his head a bit and gave her a puzzled look.

"After finding me like this, I figured you were going to think I didn't have any sense at all."

"Just because Valene was valedictorian doesn't mean you're not bright. How about if you stop comparing yourself and always thinking you come out on the short end of the deal?"

If he'd barked the words at her or teased, it would have been easier. Since his voice went so soft and earnest, she gulped.

He tugged a bit on her wrist and muttered, "You're really jammed in there."

The whole situation struck her as so ludicrous, she started to giggle. "You know me—I took that old cliché to heart. 'Anything worth doing is worth doing right.'"

Nathan's arm tightened around her. "So you're saying this was worth doing?"

How am I supposed to answer that?

The patter of Jeff's shoes saved her from having to formulate an answer. "Here's the shampoo!" He climbed over their legs and sat next to Amber. While Nathan withdrew his hand and gooped it up with the unscented liquid, Jeff scratched his knee. "What did you pray for, Van?"

She jerked on her hand once again to no avail and confessed, "Patience."

"Here goes nothing." Nathan curled back around her and slid his hand up by her wrist. "My fingers are fatter than yours. If I shove my hand any higher, we'll both get stuck. Can you wiggle your hand to the side a little?"

"Which side?"

"That way." He nudged her a bit. "Good. I'll see if I can rub some of this slimy stuff on the metal bar here and on the edge of your hand. Afterward, if you jostle your hand over here, maybe we can work just enough of the soap under the ring to make your finger slip free."

"I don't even know if it'll come off." She fidgeted, hoping to spread the shampoo around. "Grandma gave one to each of us on our thirteenth birthday."

"You've never taken it off?"

"Nope."

"Wow," Jeff said. He gave her an incredulous look. "Dad said all rings have to come off sooner or later. He keeps his in his sock drawer."

Nathan went completely still. Vanessa closed her eyes for a moment, sensing the pain that rolled off him. He'd said very little about his wife, but what he had said made it clear he'd loved her dearly. It must have been heart wrenching to finally remove his wedding band.

He drew in a deep, steadying breath. In a tight voice, he ordered, "Now try to work your hand free."

A few, very long minutes later, she felt a little give. "Almost—it slipped a little bit."

"Good." Nathan clenched her elbow. "On the count of three. One, two, three!"

He yanked, she pulled, and her hand came free.

"Oh, thank you, thank you, thank you."

"So you got what you prayed for," Jeff said as he hugged Amber.

Nathan opened the drawer, pried the ring free, and shoved it back at Vanessa. He stared at his son and rasped, "Prayers are like dreams and wishes. Not all of them come true. Don't ever forget that."

❧

At least once a week, Nathan arranged for Vanessa to work with him, Jeff, and Licorice. Every weekend, he brought Jeff to Whiskers, Wings, and Wags to buy a bag of kibble.

"I can order this in larger bags. It comes in twenty and forty pounds," Vanessa offered.

"Not a chance." Nathan plunked a ten-dollar bill onto the counter. "Don't even start down that path. You could charm a snake into buying a pedicure, but I'm impervious to this particular sales pitch."

"A pedicured snake?"

He ignored her entertained echo. "Our place is small. I don't want to have to go out to the garage or backyard to grab a scoop of chow for the little beast."

"Isn't that funny? For some odd reason, I figured a man in the construction business would have a big old house."

"Old, yes; big, no. Evie and I bought an 1865 saltbox back in Massachusetts on our honeymoon." For the first time, the memory flitted though his mind without tearing a jagged hole in his heart.

"A saltbox? How charming!"

"You wouldn't have said that if you'd have seen it. The poor thing was slated for destruction. Evie went wild over it and said all the rickety old house needed was elbow grease and love, so we had the place all numbered, dismantled, and shipped out here. I put it back together on a big lot." Under his breath, he recalled, "We always figured we could add on."

"Dad's building me a fort. A giant one with a swing set underneath."

"Neato! Are you helping?"

Nathan grinned. "He's sanding the shutters and is going to paint them."

"If you need an extra pair of hands, I'm willing to help." She lifted her arms and fluttered her fingers in the air. "A pair of nice guys rescued me, so I can offer to be useful."

"Dad's putting a zebra in the backyard. He said he'd need lotsa help with that."

"A zebra?" Vanessa gawked at him. "You really weren't kidding when you said if you got one animal, you'd end up with a menagerie!"

Nathan chuckled. "Jeff's got the wrong idea. It's a gazebo, not a zebra."

"No zebra?" His son gave him a dismayed look.

"No zebra. No cats, rats, birds, or lizards, either." He glanced about the pet shop and hoped he hadn't missed out on anything readily visible, because sure as the sun rose, if he missed something, Jeff would take that as a promise that he could have one. In the off chance he had overlooked a creature, Nathan shook his finger at his son—as much to keep his attention focused on him as anything else. "Don't press your luck. We have an agreement, and you're behind on your end of the deal."

Jeff blurted out a laugh and slapped his hand over his mouth.

"Just what is so funny?" Vanessa folded her arms on the counter and leaned forward.

"Dad made a joke about our agreement about Lick." Jeff whispered very blatant clues at a decibel only a first grader would consider secretive. "Behind. End."

Vanessa made a goofy face. "Well, Buster, you'd better clean up your act. I'm not coming over to help on a fort or a gazebo if I have to tiptoe through the tulips."

"We don't got no flowers."

"Have," Nathan corrected. "We don't have any flowers." *Evie loved flowers, and I still can't stand to tend them.* He shoved away the thought and cleared his throat. "I don't have time to mess with detailed gardening. If something needs more than routine watering and an occasional trimming, you can bet it's not in my yard."

"Juggling a thriving business, a kid, and an energetic puppy would be enough for anyone." Vanessa's lips pursed, and the impish gleam in her eyes warned Nathan he'd better prepare himself for whatever she'd say next.

"The best thing for you would be some free time. You know: recreation."

"Is that so?" he asked sardonically.

"Absolutely. Something fun. Let you get out a bit. Be with good people. Enjoy fresh air."

"Are you—" Jeff bobbed and weaved from one side of his father's long, lean legs to the other "—sending Dad to summer camp?"

"Nope." Nathan ruffled his son's hair. "I think Van's trying to rope me into playing baseball."

"Where's her rope?"

"With the zebra?" Vanessa ventured in a playful tone.

"Sport, I need a minute with Vanessa. Why don't you go see if you can spot Goldie in the fish tank?" He waited until

Jeff was out of earshot, then braced both hands on the counter. It took everything in him to keep from thundering, but he refused to lose control. "Forget it. Just forget this plan of yours to lure me back into church. I know the whole deal—sucker someone into an activity they like, then chip away the defenses until they start attending services. Well, it's not going to work, Vanessa. Not on me."

"Okay. I promise I won't ever invite you to worship. It doesn't mean you can't just have a good time with great people."

"You just don't get it, so I'm going to be blunt. My wife died. She was a devout believer. We prayed for a miracle, but she died an inch at a time of kidney failure. A good Christian man would have accepted it, but I didn't. I still haven't. Call me jaded or bitter or a backslider—I know all of the churchy terms for it. There's one thing I refuse to be, and that's a hypocrite. I'm not about to wear a mask and pretend everything is hunky-dory."

"Who said you have to?"

He slammed his fist on the counter. "I went to church the Sunday after the funeral. I needed God. I needed comfort. Instead, I ended up having to put up with half of the congregation weeping all over me. How was I supposed to console them when all I could do was look at my son and know God took away his mother?"

"I'm sorry you hurt." She slid her hand over his fist.

"What? No shock that I'd dare to be mad at God?"

Vanessa simply squeezed his clenched fist. "There's nothing wrong with being angry. God is bigger than your rage, and He's patient."

Her response caught him off guard. Embarrassed by his outburst, Nathan mumbled, "I'm not about to darken the door of a church."

"There aren't any stained-glass windows or sermons on a ball diamond." She waggled her brows. "And I'll help with your gazebo."

"You drive a hard bargain. Do you drive nails half as well?"

"Just you wait and see."

six

Vanessa sat on the edge of the deck they'd just made for the gazebo and winced as Nathan yanked a splinter from his hand. "Want some help with that?"

"Naw. It's no big deal. I get 'em all the time."

"When you said you were building a gazebo, I didn't imagine anything quite this grand."

The leather of his tool belt made a slight stretching sound, and some of the tools clinked together as he laid back and supported himself on his elbows. He gave her a taunting grin. "In over your head?"

"I'm holding my own." She gave him a saucy smile. "Except for when it comes to tools. Your cordless power stuff is really nifty."

"Occupational benefit."

"Oh, come on. Who are you kidding? Even if you weren't in the construction business, you'd still have the biggest and best power tools made because they're big boys' toys."

"I collect toys; you collect things with fur, fins, or feathers. From where I sit, it seems like you shouldn't be throwing rocks since you're living in a glass house."

"From where you sit?" Her ponytail swished impudently as she gawked around at the gazebo. "I might have glass walls to my so-called house, but this little house of yours has none at all!"

"Just you wait and see." He stood and pulled her to her feet. "This baby's going to be done in no time at all."

She picked up a drill, slipped her forefinger through the trigger loop, and made it whine. "Thanks to these toys."

"And thanks to you. It's a lot easier getting things done with an extra pair of hands."

"I'm having fun." She turned to go back to work. "We ought to be able to get the main beams up and the benches made today."

"I'm amazed. I thought Amber would go nuts over the whine of the drill. She just curls up out of the way, and the noise doesn't even faze her."

"It's all part of training her to ignore things. I've taken her to construction sites, parades, and high school basketball and football games. She's learned that noise, vibration, and movement aren't as important as being a good girl." Vanessa stroked Amber approvingly. "It's all a part of learning good puppy manners, and you are a perfect lady, aren't you?"

"Incredible. Why doesn't she stretch out?"

"That's part of her training too. We teach the dogs to 'be small.' She's going to have to fit under seats on a bus, ride in a plane and train, and be in auditoriums. If she stretches out, someone will step on her, or she'll become an obstacle."

"How'd you learn all of this?"

"There's a manual, and I go to puppy-raiser meetings twice a month."

"Meetings? What do you do?"

"One meeting is usually a combination business and obediencetraining meeting. The second one is normally an outing. We take the puppies somewhere so they can be exposed to a challenging environment or situation and learn how to respond appropriately. It's a great group of people and dogs."

She reached over for another length of wood he'd already cut to size. "If you have any wood left over, you could make a doghouse for Lick."

"Why bother? He's sleeping in Jeff's room."

"I know we're in California, but it does rain every once in awhile."

Nathan waved his hand to indicate the gazebo. "And this isn't enough shelter?"

"That all depends."

"On what?

She gave him a look of owl-eyed innocence. "If you like eau de wet puppy."

"Okay. I'm convinced. A doghouse is my next project."

"Then we'd better get back to work and finish this up."

A few hours later, they took another breather.

"This yard is huge." Vanessa scanned. "I'll bet you have a cool lawn mower."

"It all depends on what you think is cool. I hired the kid next door to mow and edge. He wanted to earn money for football."

"He's probably rich enough to own the team by now. What is this—an acre?"

"Three-quarters of an acre. I tried to keep the gazebo to scale. It would have looked pretty ridiculous to have one of those little scaled-down jobs back here."

"Yeah, well, Jeff's fort is so big, I'm expecting the U.S. Navy to billet a few officers in it."

Nathan bent his head over his palm and plucked out another splinter as he mumbled, "Jeff wanted the extra level and the rope netting. It wasn't that much more work."

"Did you really camp out up there last Friday?"

"Yup. Lanterns, sleeping bags, and mosquitoes." He turned toward the house and yelled, "Jeff, where's that lemonade?"

The door opened. Jeff stuck his head out and shouted, "I can't reach the glasses."

"Aren't there clean ones in the dishwasher?"

"Huh-unh. We forgot to run it. I can tell 'cuz there's still pasgetti on the plates."

"I'll go help him." Vanessa sprang to her feet. Amber accompanied her across the lawn and into the house. The minute she got inside, Vanessa sucked in a deep breath. She'd never seen Nathan's house.

Clearly, a busy man, a little boy, and an undisciplined puppy lived here. School papers cluttered the refrigerator door and the coffee table. Both the telephone and the stove bore spaghetti sauce splatters, and a small bulletin board listed two baby-sitters, several fast-food places, and a few scrawled memos. Two pair of muddy shoes—one small, the other huge—sat on the hearth, and a track of muddy paw prints zigzagged down the hall.

"The glasses are up there." Jeff pointed to a cupboard on the right side of the sink.

Vanessa opened it and spied a set of earthenware dishes adorned with pinkish flowers around the edges. It seemed so absurdly feminine in a father-and-son home, but that fact tugged at her heart. Clearly, Nathan still held his wife's memory dear, and he clung to the little things that still kept her alive in his heart. She must've been someone very special.

Bypassing the glass tumblers in favor of three mismatched plastic cups, Vanessa said, "These look like good ones to take to the backyard."

"I'll pour the lemonade."

"Okay." She fought the urge to take over. Nathan encouraged Jeff to be independent, and it wouldn't hurt anything if they had to wipe up a spill. She took the time to scan the house a bit more.

A woman's touch was still very evident. Wallpaper of dainty sprays of antique roses covered the far side of the kitchen, echoed by linoleum flooring that held a pattern of tiles with little rose-colored flowers. A five-foot-long pine board hung from the ceiling. Several decorator-quality baskets dangled from pegs on it.

"Forgive the mess," a deep voice said from behind her.

Vanessa jumped at that sound. "It's a wonderful place."

"Consuelo will be back on Monday. She's spending a week visiting her sister. She manages to keep Jeff out of trouble when he gets home from school and keeps the place from being a total pit. Three days on our own, and we've just about demolished the downstairs. Jeff and I were going to pick up a bit before you got here, but—"

"We got busy watching cartoons," Jeff interrupted.

Vanessa watched red creep up Nathan's neck. "Don't be embarrassed. I did the same thing. I was supposed to be sorting through the pots and pans, but I ate my cereal in front of the TV and got stuck on good old *Rocky and Bullwinkle* reruns."

Nathan swiped two of the glasses from the counter and handed her one. "*Rocky and Bullwinkle*, huh?"

"My favorite."

"So even as a kid, you had a thing for animals."

"Guilty as charged." She took a sip. "Great lemonade, Jeff."

"Thanks. Can the dogs drink some too?"

"No," Nathan and Vanessa said in unison.

"Why not?"

Nathan looked at Vanessa. "You're the expert."

"People food isn't always healthy for dogs. Every once in awhile, if your dad lets you, you can give Lick some of your leftovers."

"Oh, great," Jeff sighed. "Dad always finishes everything. We don't got no leftovers."

"We don't have any leftovers," Nathan corrected.

"That's what I said. Poor Licorice is gonna starve!"

Vanessa walked out of the kitchen and into the backyard before she burst into laughter.

A short while later, Nathan pounded one last nail into a board and asked, "Why are you sorting pots and pans?"

"Valene bought a condo. We're trying to decide who owns what."

"You mean the Dynamic Duo is splitting up?"

"Hard to imagine, isn't it? Actually, I think it's a great move—pardon the pun. Val landed a job in the business office at the hospital. The condo is close, so she won't have to worry about a long commute."

"It's not all that far—about twenty minutes or so?"

"Close enough to still meet and go to church and do things together."

"Outgoing as you are, you'll stay busy." He stuffed the hammer into his tool belt without even looking. "Aren't you worried Val will feel a bit lost?"

"I think it'll be a good change for her—she'll need a little nudging, but she'll make friends. If anything, I'm going to be lost without her. She's so organized and capable."

"Capable? Look at you, Van. You own and run a store. You have an active social life. You're great at sports, volunteer in the community, and are better with a hammer and saw than half of the men I hire. Don't sell yourself short."

She looked into his coffee brown eyes and saw the sincerity there. His praise meant more to her than it probably ought to. Uncomfortable with the sudden closeness she felt, she wiped her palms on the sides of her jeans. "If I do something stupid like forgetting to pay the electricity bill so I lose my power, I'm going to sneak over and sleep in Jeff's fort."

Concern creased Nathan's forehead. "You're used to splitting rent. Are you going to be in trouble?"

"No, Val wouldn't ever leave me in the lurch. The shop's doing well. I can afford to live alone. Amber's good company, too, aren't you, Girl?"

Amber wagged her tail.

Nathan looked across the yard at Jeff and Lick as they tumbled in the grass. "Any chance you'll train him to sit quietly?"

"Are you asking about Jeff or Licorice?"

"Hey. For that, I'm not going to volunteer to help Val move."

seven

"Just how much stuff have the two of you squirreled away in this place?" Nathan took in the pile of boxes and blinked in disbelief.

"This place has a lot of storage space," Valene murmured as she glanced about the apartment.

"She's only taking her stuff." Vanessa capped the black marker with a flourish after she finished writing "Kitchen—dishes. Breakable!" on a box.

"Not really. Vanessa's giving me a bunch of things that probably are rightfully hers."

"It's really an excuse for me to go buy new dishes. I want to get something different."

The shuffle of booted feet at the doorway made them all turn. "Kip! You came." Vanessa waved him in. "I nearly fought Val to the death so I could keep the coffeemaker. There's a fresh pot in the kitchen, if either of you men need to get juiced up with caffeine before we start."

"What? No doughnuts?" Kip crossed the room and slapped Nathan on the shoulder in greeting. "These two women are going to work us half to death, then let starvation complete the job."

"I suppose this is my cue to say something like, 'I made Grandma's cinnamon coffee cake,' but I probably ought to confess that Valene is taking the couch."

Nathan stared at the big, pale blue, fluffy-cushioned couch and rubbed his forehead. "How about if I go for the coffee, cake, and no couch?"

Kip flopped down on the couch. "You've obviously never tasted Vanessa's cooking! Me? I'll take the coffee and move the couch. I've tasted something she made once. Believe me, once was more than enough. It wasn't fit for human consumption."

"Hey!" Vanessa tossed the marker at him and headed into the kitchen. "Just because you don't know dog food when you see it. . ."

"Dog food?" Nathan looked from Kip to Valene for an explanation.

A shy smile lit Valene's face. "Van made special biscuits for Mrs. Culpepper's poodle. She's got heart problems and needs low sodium treats."

"It was Valentine's Day," Kip groused. "How was I supposed to know they weren't heart-shaped cookies? She had them on a plate!"

Van came back into the room. She balanced four mismatched holiday paper plates that held plastic forks and big, fragrant chunks of pastry.

Nathan happily swiped one, handed it to Valene, and took one for himself as Kip scrambled off the couch and dove for another. "Wow. I thought you were kidding when you said something about your granny's recipe."

"It's not cinnamon; it's her lemon cream cheese loaf," Vanessa said.

Nathan took a bite. It melted in his mouth. He quickly licked a pastry crumb off his lip. "For this, I'll even help move the couch."

"Careful." Kip gave a wary look around the boxes. "They're bribing us. There's got to be a catch somewhere." His eyes narrowed. "Val, is your new condo an upstairs one?"

"Not a chance. By the time I get home from a four-mile run, I don't want to have to jog up the stairs."

Kip chuckled. "And I thought you were going to tell us Vanessa is afraid of heights."

Nathan gulped down the last bite of pastry and shook his head. "Vanessa is fearless."

She bumped into a stack of boxes and quoted, "I can do all things through Him who strengthens me."

"Then why did you want us to come help you move all of this junk?"

The move only took the morning hours. Valene had everything organized and ready to go, and the men managed to wedge everything into the truck she'd rented. After a single trip, they'd hauled everything out and taken it into Val's new place. The twins' parents were out of town, but they called from their hotel and arranged for a local deli to furnish lunch. A four-foot submarine sandwich with all of the trimmings was delivered just as Nathan wheeled in a dolly with the last stack of boxes on it.

As they ate, Kip tossed a can of soda to Nathan and said, "We still have a spot for you on the team."

"I'm not going to church."

Vanessa startled at the vehemence of his tone.

Kip shrugged. "I didn't invite you to church. Course you're welcome if you wanna come, but I'm talking about home plate, not the offering plate."

Aware he'd startled Vanessa and Valene, Nathan felt a niggling of guilt. He pushed it aside. There was nothing wrong with a man standing firm on an issue. Then again, there was nothing wrong with a guy playing ball, either. "Okay, here's the deal: I'll play. But don't expect me to warm a pew."

"We're in business."

"Business!" Vanessa glanced at her watch. "I have to mind the shop for a couple of hours. Jamie could only stay 'til two today. I'll be back at about six to help you unpack the boxes, Val." She hugged her sister, dashed for the door, and sang over her shoulder, "Thanks for lugging all of my sissy's stuff, guys!"

❧

Vanessa sailed back through her sister's door at a few minutes after six.

"Next time I get a great idea and decide to move," Valene sighed as she plopped down on the couch, "shoot me."

Vanessa stepped around a stack of towels, clung to a large roasting pan with oven mitts, and looked around the living room. "You've unpacked almost half of the boxes! We'll finish up later. For now. . ."

Valene gave her a weary smile. "Supper. Whatever it is, I'll eat it."

"Here you are." Vanessa set the roasting pan on the bare coffee table.

"Put the mitts under that! I don't want the wood ruined!"

Vanessa ignored her twin and lifted the lid with a flourish. "Ta da!"

"What in the world?" Val leaned forward and stared at the pan. Nestled inside was a cell phone with a colorful rectangle of paper taped to the bottom. She lifted the phone, and Vanessa started to laugh as Valene tore off the coupon and read aloud, "Free pizza?"

"But of course. Home delivery. And observe, Mam'selle. . ." She pulled out a red-and-white-checkered plastic tablecloth, spread it on the coffee table, and topped it with matching paper plates and napkins she'd stuffed into the roasting pan. "You go ahead and call. I already arranged for them to bring a large pizza with the works, soda, and salad."

"What? No dessert?"

Vanessa gave her a wounded look. "Have you ever known me to skimp on the essentials?" She pulled a small gold box of chocolate truffles from the roasting pan and set it in the center of the table with all due consideration.

"Perfect. How about if we eat those while we wait for the pizza?"

"Be still, my beating heart!" Vanessa patted her chest theatrically. "Is that my always-sensible twin sister suggesting something that decadent?"

"I am being sensible. If I turn my back, you'll eat the hazelnut." She leaned forward, lifted the foil box's lid, and plucked out her favorite. After she called for the pizza, she crossed one leg beneath her on the sofa and made direct eye contact. "I want to talk to you for a minute about being sensible."

"Uh-oh. You just pasted on your serious look."

"I am serious. Van, Nathan is a troubled man. He's really resistant to anything having to do with God."

"I know." She stared at her sister and sighed. "What kind of Christian would I be to reject him instead of coming alongside him? He's mad at God. Really mad. I've been there too. Remember when Grandma died? I hurt so badly, I didn't pray all summer."

"Yeah, but from what Kip said, Nathan's been bitter for years now."

"Nathan hasn't made any secret of it. God is patient, Val. I figure we can either push Nathan away, or we can draw him back to the Lord. It's not something that will be fixed overnight. Baby steps—it's a matter of baby steps. You heard him—he'll join the team."

"Don't fall for him, Van. It'll break your heart."

eight

Nathan peeked in on Jeff. His son was sprawled across the bed sideways, the pillow lay on the floor, and the puppy was curled up at the head of the bed where the pillow belonged. Letting out a sigh, Nathan crossed the hardwood floor. His footsteps made a solid sound, but he doubted a full-volume Sousa march would rouse Jeff. Licorice's head lifted, and his tail made a rapid *whump, whump, whump* against the oak headboard.

"You don't belong up here." Nathan planned to scoop the puppy off the bed, place him on the floor, and have him trot out to the back door for one last pit stop. Once he reached for the dog, his plans altered.

Licorice's tongue darted out and lapped at Nathan's wrist. The speed of his tail wagging a drumbeat against the headboard doubled. Nathan picked him up, cradled him in his arms, and left the room. As he walked down the hall and reached the squeaky third step on the stairs, the puppy squirmed and snuffled until his little wet nose nudged at the base of Nathan's throat.

Nathan stopped on the stairs and looked down. "I'm Granite Cliffs's biggest pushover, you know. You're the living proof of that. If you weren't so cute, it would be downright embarrassing that I put up with you."

The small metal tags on Lick's collar jingled.

"Yeah. I know." Nathan carried him down the rest of the stairs, through the living room, and out the kitchen door.

He put down the pooch and sat out in the gazebo. It was too early to turn in, and he had too many thoughts running though his mind to bother trying to follow a plot of any television show.

He took up a piece of sandpaper and started to rub out a small ding on the right edge of the western bench in the gazebo. After a few passes, his action halted. He didn't want to make that nick disappear.

Vanessa had been hammering trellis on the side of the gazebo, and her hammer slipped. She'd been upset about the blemish in the bench, but it was such a minor imperfection, Nathan knew he could sand it smooth. For now, he'd still leave that nick there—it was like a reminder of the golden afternoon when they'd constructed this.

Vanessa. He'd felt a spurt of emotion when Kip showed up at her apartment this morning to help with the move. Were they dating? The thought turned his stomach. He had no right to be jealous or possessive. None whatsoever. He and Vanessa were. . .*what are we?*

He couldn't exactly answer that nagging question. When Kip said he hadn't had any of Vanessa's cooking other than the dog biscuits, that had made Nathan breathe a little easier. As they'd all worked together to carry things out to the moving truck and haul them into Valene's new place, Nathan noticed Kip kept mixing up the sisters.

They both wore blue jeans and old, faded red Whiskers, Wings, and Wags T-shirts. Other than that, Kip must have been hit in the head with one too many wild pitches if he thought Van and Val were interchangeable. Val was a pretty young woman; Van was ravishingly beautiful. She just plain sparkled. Her moves carried an exuberance and grace that captivated Nathan.

They didn't even smell alike. Val wore something from one

of those fancy bottles she'd carried into her new place in a basket; Vanessa would have given Carmen Miranda stiff competition in the fruit bowl category. Her hair smelled of strawberry shampoo, she chewed watermelon bubble gum, and when she sat beside him in the truck, she'd slicked peach gloss on her lips.

If all else failed, Kip could have just glanced down and seen that Amber shadowed Vanessa everywhere she went. *Well, maybe that isn't entirely true,* Nathan admitted to himself. *Amber stays with Valene when Vanessa is on the ball diamond.*

Licorice woofed softly. He'd grown appreciably in the past month. He'd barely been able to make it up a step that first day. Now, he undulated like a playful dolphin as he bounded up the four risers into the gazebo. Nathan groaned.

"Lick, is that mud on your nose and paws?"

Licorice skidded to a halt, leaving telltale streaks in his wake.

"What did you dig up this time?"

The puppy sank down, buried his muzzle in his paws, and made a pitiful, guilty whimper.

"Looks like I'm going to have to consult with Vanessa about what to do with a naughty little digger." Nathan leaned down and petted Lick's sleek black coat. In truth, he wasn't overly upset. It provided another good excuse to be with Vanessa again.

❧

"Do you have time for a puppy consultation?"

Vanessa clamped the receiver between her ear and her shoulder as she considered Nathan's question. She had her hands full, but she didn't want to miss what he had to say. "Uh-oh. What's Lick up to now?"

"Outsmarting me."

She didn't try to muffle her laughter. "Again?"

Silence on his end of the line might have meant he was offended, but when he spoke, his voice sounded more like he was chuckling than chiding. "You could be a little more sympathetic."

"Actually, I'm thinking how fortunate you are. Obviously Lick is a highly intelligent dog, so once he's trained, he's going to be a dream boat."

"Right about now, I'd settle for a leaky canoe."

"Well, he's a puppy, so I can guarantee he's still leaky."

"You did warn me that you'd been class clown," Nathan muttered wryly.

"Let me put Nero down so I can hold the phone." She set aside the receiver, placed the black Lab puppy she'd just groomed into an enclosure, and came back. "Thanks for waiting."

"Let me get this straight," Nathan said with a tinge of amusement. "You're fiddling with Nero while my Rome is burning."

"That's about the size of it. He and Lick are from the same litter. The family who took him didn't check with their landlord, and they've been told they'll be evicted if they keep him."

"And I thought I had problems."

"It's really no problem at all. Valene is a little lonely. She's used to me and a dog, so I've decided to give Nero to her."

"She doesn't have a yard."

"No, she doesn't. For just about anyone else, I'd encourage them to have a smaller dog if it's going to be a house pet. Val loves to walk and jog. If anything, Nero will get plenty of exercise and provide an extra measure of safety for Val. Anyway, enough about Nero and Val. What do you need?"

"Help. I'm desperate. I tell you what: Jeff and I will bring Lick to baseball practice tonight. We'll snag some Picnicin'

Chicken on the way. If we get to your shop right as it closes, we can eat in the park, and you can give me some pointers on what to do with the puppy."

"Sounds great. Feed Lick before you come—otherwise, he's going to want people food."

"Okay. Gotcha. Good tactic. See you later."

≈

Van and Amber were standing outside the pet shop when Nathan drove up. He drew alongside the curb and parked.

"There they are!" Jeff scrambled out of his seat belt and twisted to unlatch Lick from his puppy seat belt. The windows were rolled down, and he shouted, "We brought chicken and hot cherry flipovers for dessert!"

"Turnovers, Sport." Nathan identified with Jeff's eager scramble to get out of the car. Clearly, if he and Vanessa did decide to pursue a relationship, he wouldn't have to worry whether Jeff liked her. Nathan got out of the car, grabbed the rustling plastic bag holding their supper, and snatched his mitt from the dashboard.

"All set?" Vanessa stooped and paid generous attention to Lick.

"You betcha." Jeff gawked around. "Dad said you gots another dog just like mine. Where is he?"

"I do have another puppy that's Licorice's brother. I left him in the shop, and I want to keep him a big surprise. I'm giving him to Valene after the game tonight. Can you keep it a secret?"

"Yep!" Jeff hopped in place.

Nathan tilted his head and slanted his eyes toward the clouds as he shrugged, hoping Vanessa would understand his meaning. Six-year-old boys weren't exactly reliable when it came to keeping confidences.

Vanessa's eyes twinkled with understanding. She rose and lifted an electric blue athletic bag.

"I'll take that." Nathan reached for it.

"Then put your glove inside. No use carrying a bunch of loose gear." She unzipped it and opened the flaps.

Nathan made a show of leaning forward and peering inside the bag. "You don't have a python in there that'll eat my all-time favorite mitt, do you?"

She let out a theatrical sigh. "I knew I forgot something!"

"Good thing. You'd be in big trouble if anything happened to my glove. I worked at a Christmas-tree lot my sophomore year of high school so I could earn enough money for it."

"Ah, yes." She gave him a pert smile. "The old sweeter-'cuz-I-earned-it item. Val and I shared our biggie, but I suppose that wouldn't come as any surprise."

"As different as you are from one another, it is. So tell me—what did the two of you want so badly?"

"A sound system for our bedroom. When we moved to our apartment, it was the only thing in the living room."

He dropped his mitt inside. As she zipped up the bag, he mused, "It didn't occur to me until now, but you don't have any snakes in the shop."

"Snakes are icky," Jeff declared.

"Val and my mom agree with you. The day I signed the papers for this shop, they made a point of telling me not to count on their help if I kept a single snake on the premises."

As he lifted the bag of gear, Nathan asked, "It's not much of a sacrifice, is it? You already offer a wide array of animals."

"I couldn't possibly handle snakes. They don't have wings or whiskers, and they don't wag. Are we ready to go?"

"Ready!" Jeff and Nathan declared in unison.

Jeff trotted ahead with Lick sort of trying to stay at heel. The two of them tangled about every third step, but that rated as a definite improvement.

Nathan stood to Van's right so Amber could walk at heel.

With the supper bag in one hand and the athletic bag over the opposite shoulder, he didn't have a free hand. For a fleeting moment, he considered switching the picnic to his right hand so his left hand would be free to hold hers, but he dismissed that concept as soon as it flashed though his mind. He wasn't ready to jump into anything deep yet, and she seemed comfortable with matters as they stood. Most of him accepted that fact, but he still felt a twinge. He hadn't realized how lonely he'd become until he'd met Vanessa.

Laughter bubbled out of her as she watched Jeff and Lick. That sound acted like a breeze, shoving away his gloomy clouds of thoughts. Nathan started to do something he hadn't done in years.

nine

As they strolled down the street, Nathan started to whistle. It felt right, just puckering up and letting loose a stream of notes. It wasn't until they were waiting at the light that he realized what tune he'd chosen.

Vanessa said the title just as his own awareness dawned. " 'How Much Is That Doggy in the Window?' "

He gave her a sheepish look. "I guess I'd better be careful not to give away the secret, either."

Jeff took his hand before they crossed the street. "I 'membered to look both ways."

"Good going."

"Dad, did you tell on Lick?"

He squeezed Jeff's hand. "Vanessa needs to know what Licorice is doing so she can help us make him a better puppy. She's not going to stop liking him just because he did something bad."

"Like the way you still love me, even when I done wrong?"

"Do wrong. And yes, just like I will always love you, no matter what you do. Still, that's not an excuse for you to do bad things. When you love someone, you try your hardest to do things that please them."

"Then everybody is happy. Right, Dad?"

"Right."

They reached the other side of the street, and Jeff shook free from his grasp. "We'll run over to the big tree. Can we sit under the tree for our picnic?"

Nathan shot Vanessa a quick look. "Wouldn't you rather sit

at one of the picnic tables?"

"How about if we sit at a table under a tree? I don't mind sitting on the ground, but Lick is going to help himself to the food if it's down at his level. It's not fair to tempt him. He's too young to know better."

After they were seated and had started eating, Vanessa peeked under the table and asked Licorice, "So are they going to tell me what you did this time?"

"He dug a hole—a great big hole." Jeff drew a sizable circle in the air with his drumstick.

"Hmm."

"I read a few suggestions on-line," Nathan confessed. "I tried two of them. Both were abysmal failures."

"What did you do?"

"I blew up a balloon, put it in the hole, and covered it with dirt. Supposedly the loud pop was supposed to be a deterrent. The only thing it did was send him running to another spot, where he promptly started digging a new hole."

"Persistent little monster, isn't he?"

Nathan thought her voice held a blend of sympathy for him and a tad of amusement. He broke eye contact and scooped in a few hefty bites of coleslaw.

"So what else have you tried?"

"A squirt gun!" Jeff guffawed.

Nathan gave Vanessa his if-you-can't-beat-'em-join-'em grin. "We discovered Lick loves water. Silly animal came charging toward me and tried to drink from the Super Squirtmaster."

"So I gotta Squirtmaster to play with now." Jeff's delight couldn't be more clear.

"So much for my foray into effective canine discipline."

"Labs are water dogs." Vanessa took a quick sip of soda and set the can back onto the sun-bleached wooden tabletop. "The nice thing is, he'll love going to the beach with you."

"If he digs there," Nathan grumbled, "maybe he'll fall all of the way through to China."

"Dad! You wouldn't let that happen, would you?"

"No, he was just teasing, Jeff. There are some things you can do to stop the digging. If you play with him more and tire him out, he won't have the energy to dig. There are a few products out on the market that keep a dog from digging, and you can spray them on the ground in a few key places where the digging will destroy special plants."

"Okay. I know the shop is already closed, but can I go ahead and pick up some of that tonight?"

"Sure." She slanted him a questioning look. "Have you been gardening?"

"Yeah. How'd you guess?"

"He planted flowers." Jeff's little body swayed back and forth in cadence with how he swung his legs. "But Lick dug most all of 'em up."

Vanessa's brows arched in surprise. "I thought you said you weren't much on flowers."

"A certain person who helped me build the gazebo pointed out the backyard would look a lot better if I planted some."

Her brows wiggled as she did a truly pathetic Groucho Marx imitation. "I'll bet that person was right."

"Who knows? The little black beast made mulch of them."

Vanessa rested her forearms on the picnic table and leaned forward. Her voice softened. "Nathan, Lick saw you digging in the dirt. He thought it was okay. Until he gets older, you'd do well not to set an example you don't want him to follow."

"Oh, brother! Do I feel stupid!"

"Now I'll make you feel downright smart: Go get some chicken wire. Put about an inch of dirt over it, and just comb flower seeds into the soil. He won't be able to dig, and you'll only spend a fraction of what you would for pony packs of flowers."

"For that, you deserve a cherry turnover."

❧

That Friday, after the game, Vanessa gathered her gear and collected Amber from Val. "Wanna go out for some ice cream?"

"Double fudge?"

"Double dips," Vanessa promised.

Deep laughter from behind them made her turn around. Nathan rested his hands on his hips. "Double scoops of double fudge for twins. Don't tell me you don't see the humor in that."

"Dad, can we get ice cream too?"

Vanessa saw the question in Nathan's eyes. "Sure, you guys can come along. We'll sit outside the shop so Nero and Lick can come along."

Jeff knelt between the two Lab puppies. Both turned as if on cue and licked him. "What about Amber? Won't she come?"

"Amber is allowed to go into most places like church and restaurants and stores because she's a service animal."

"Sis?"

Vanessa turned to Val. "Huh?"

"I hope you don't mind, but I changed his name. Nero was a madman, and I wanted something a little more. . .noble."

"I don't care one bit. What did you decide on?"

"Hero."

"Oh, that was clever. I'll bet he's responding to it right away."

Valene beamed. "He is. He's so bright. I want him to start in with the next session of puppy obedience. When does it start?"

"Next Saturday."

Nathan knelt and scratched both Lick and Hero behind the ears. "Did you boys hear that? You're going to be classmates."

"Can they have ice cream too, to cel'brate? You taked me out for ice cream when I started school."

"I don't know." Nathan looked up at her. "You didn't let us feed the dogs at our picnic."

"Amber eats twice a day. I give her treats, but not while I'm eating or socializing, because I don't want her to turn into a beggar."

Val hitched the strap of her purse higher on her shoulder. "We probably ought to use the same system we did back when you had Thane."

Vanessa nodded and explained to Nathan and Jeff, "I had my first guide puppy in my senior year of high school. We still had our family dog, a poodle named Fluffy. Fluffy wanted treats like she used to get—she was pretty spoiled. We taught the dogs that Fluffy got a treat when Thane got to go on an outing."

"Then I guess going on the trip is enough. Lick won't get a lick of ice cream."

Jeff giggled. "That was funny, Dad."

"Ice cream?" Kip sauntered up. "Are you going out for ice cream? I'm inviting myself along."

As they sat on the little wrought-iron patio set outside of the ice cream parlor, she watched Nathan wipe a dab of Very Berry from Jeff's face. He looked up at Vanessa just as she realized a little chocolate had dripped on her chin. He beat Kip to the stack of napkins in the center of the table and handed one to her. "So you got your first dog in high school. Why?"

"I love animals, and it seemed like a neat thing to do. Since we'd be in college in a year, it wasn't right for me to get a dog of my own and leave it behind with my folks."

"That makes sense, but then I'm running into a logic problem. You told me this is your fourth guide puppy, so you had to have a dog or two while you were in college."

"I listed puppy training on my college application under community service. The college admissions officer noticed it and mentioned that he'd give me clearance to have a puppy in classes as long as we didn't have any major accidents or disruptions."

"Did you?"

"Mom does a lot of volunteer work, and Dad was able to take the dogs to work with him at the phone company some days. Between Val and me juggling class schedules and our folks filling in, we breezed through college with the pups. Our first dog, Thane, was the biggest challenge. He was a riot."

Val choked back a giggle. "He about caused a riot on more than one occasion. The poor thing pitched a full-scale fit the first time he spied you in your shark suit. She came into the auditorium for a school assembly, and I think Thane thought the shark had eaten her."

"If Val hadn't let go of the leash, it wouldn't have been such a disaster. It took all but one member of the football team to catch Thane." Vanessa ignored her sister's don't-you-dare look and added, "The quarterback was a little preoccupied, flirting with my sister."

"Which is why she'd let go of the leash?" Nathan ventured as he gave Val a knowing grin. "Can't fault a man for having good taste."

"Sure can't," Kip agreed in a hearty tone.

"Thanks, guys—but you'll notice, my sister had the full attention of the rest of the team."

"Yeah," Vanessa snorted. "And who wouldn't, dressed up like a huge stuffed shark with a growling puppy clamped onto the fin?"

"What did you do?" Jeff wondered as several rivulets of ice cream ran down the cone, onto his hand.

"Yeah, Van," Kip nudged her arm. "What did you do?"

"A very funny dance," Val answered. "You started this, Van, so I'm telling the rest of the story. The dog wouldn't let go of the shark, and the shark kept running in a circle and wouldn't let go of the dog. There's a great picture of it in our yearbook as one of the football players took a dive toward them. The caption is BAIT AND TACKLE. "

"Oh, well," Vanessa laughed. "What do I say? She's brainy, and I'm zany. I think I keep her guardian angel and mine busy enough for both of us."

"My mom is with the angels." Jeff's comment immediately changed the focus of the conversation.

"Then she's in a very happy place."

Vanessa heard her sister's sweet words as she watched Nathan wrap his arm around Jeff's shoulders. "That's right, Son." His action bespoke support and love, yet he didn't let anyone give him that same comfort.

If he were a puppy or a kitten, she would have known a score of ways to coax him to draw close and let her give comfort. Originally he'd seemed bitter; now he had become matter-of-fact, like someone who woodenly recited a rote prayer but the meaning behind the words didn't register. Nathan built walls and constructed defenses she couldn't begin to get beyond. Until he was ready, no one would be able to reach him. All she could do was pray the Lord would work in his heart. . .and trust that when the time was right, God would have someone there to show His comfort and consolation to Nathan.

ten

Nathan sat in the shady courtyard with five other puppy owners. Had anyone asked, he would have said Vanessa looked like a luscious slice of lemon meringue pie, dressed in her crisp yellow walking shorts and a gauzy white blouse. He watched Vanessa demonstrate the simple commands she'd be working on with the "puppy kindergarten" members. Amber obediently followed each order.

"Just how long before Marzipan does all of those tricks?" one woman asked.

The burly man next to Nathan tried to untangle his beagle's leash from around his own legs and muttered, "Right about now, I'd settle for this mutt learning to sit. I'm going to fall and break my neck if Soupy keeps running circles around me."

After the session was over, folks wandered into Whiskers, Wings, and Wags to make some purchases. Jamie, the clerk who had been minding the store, slipped out for her lunch break. Nathan saw several other customers browsing too.

"What if I hang out with Hero and Licorice for awhile in one of the enclosures so Val can help you out?"

One desperate glance at the line at the register, and Van gave him a grateful smile. "Bless you!"

Nathan watched the puppies frolic and listened to Vanessa's cheerful voice as she helped her customers. Her zest for life appealed to him. She was every bit as sunny and bouncy as her hair.

For the past five years, he'd had a deep shadow of grief over his life. Evie begged him not to run from life, to feel free to fall in love again. "God has someone special in store for you and Jeff. I have an assurance about that."

He'd shaken his head. He didn't want any other woman. Since Evie died, not a day went by that he hadn't looked around the home they'd lovingly restored and missed her. . . until he met Vanessa. Oh, there had been plenty of beautiful women who made it abundantly clear they'd be happy to be the new Mrs. Adams. Not one of them deserved a second look or thought.

How could it be? In one slim month, Vanessa crashed right through all of his defenses. One month? One day. That very first day he'd been here, he'd changed. Nathan could hardly imagine it, but now he was sitting on the floor, two little black Labs playing with his shoelaces, and feeling perfectly content to hear Vanessa talk to old Mrs. Rosetti about the lamb-and-rice dog biscuits.

A father couldn't exactly dive into dating and courtship. Nathan resolved to take things slowly. He had Jeff to think of. Then again, he needed to kick things up a few notches. The thought that Vanessa and Kip might be an item had had him in knots. Now that he knew this wasn't the case, he wanted to be smart enough to start reeling her in. He wasn't about to sit back and let another man steal his sunshine.

"Who are your pals?"

Nathan didn't have to look up to identify the speaker. "Val, if you can't recognize your own four-legged kid, your sister's going to disown you."

She laughed. "It wouldn't be the first time she's been tempted."

He clipped a leash back onto Hero's collar, lifted him over the hip-high wall, and placed him in Val's arms. "Jeff's hoping you'll bring Hero to the park next Thursday for our baseball practice. He thinks the brothers need to play together."

"Smart kid you have there." Vanessa refilled the treat jar by the enclosure. "Puppies need to socialize so they learn to get along well."

Val agreed to the plan and left, but Nathan found he wasn't eager to go. He sauntered to the front of the shop and watched as Vanessa deftly straightened up a display of squeaky toys. He liked that about her—she managed to keep things tidy without making a big fuss or to-do about it.

"Do you think I'll ever manage to train Lick to be as obedient as Amber is?"

"I think you have an excellent start." She gave him a hundred-watt smile. "You have to remember I've worked with Amber for ten months. She was only eight weeks old when I got her, so we've had plenty of time to develop rapport. Several months from now, you and Lick will be a great team."

"Yeah, but probably not like you and Amber. You're with her twenty-four/seven."

"That bonding and intense teamwork do pay off. I won't pretend otherwise, but the world is full of well-behaved dogs that haven't been with their owners any more than you're with Lick."

"I hope you're right. I watched Val, and she seems to have Hero well in control—much better than I do Lick, and I've had him longer."

Vanessa's eyes twinkled. "She was moaning about how much better you are with Lick."

"No kidding?"

"It's the absolute truth. Everyone wants a cute little fluff ball, but they forget that the little guys have to learn the rules of the home, just like a child would. The first month with a puppy is always challenging. As of this week, you've passed that mark. You've had him for five weeks. Things ought to start improving a lot."

Her words carried the assurance he sought, but he wanted to keep visiting. Nathan shifted his weight and wondered, "Are you as hungry as I am?"

"I'm starving. Why?"

"Two reasons. First, because I thought we could go snag a burger. The second is, I think it's going to be a persistent issue after these Saturday classes."

"Why would that be?"

"Because every last dog in the class is named after food!"

Vanessa tickled a kitten through a cage and mused aloud, "Oh? I didn't even notice. There was Marzipan. And Pepper."

"I've got Licorice, and that guy next to me had Soupy. The English pug is Cheerio."

"But Val's dog is Hero. It doesn't—"

"Hero sandwich," Nathan reminded her.

Vanessa's laughter pealed through the air. "Know what? I limit the class to six. I had another request that I slotted for the next series: 'Brownie.'"

"So what do you say? Jamie ought to be coming back from her lunch break soon. She can hold down the fort while we fill up after our brainwashing ordeal."

"What about Lick?"

Oops. Blew it on that account. Nathan tapped the toe of his athletic shoe on the linoleum floor, then grinned. "How about if he takes a nap in the grooming room?"

"Poor baby. Is he plumb tuckered out after his first day of puppy kindergarten?"

"Yes, but his daddy is trying to get on the teacher's good side by offering to take her out for lunch."

"I always thought you were supposed to take the teacher an apple."

"Oh, that's for teachers who have children for their pupils. Dogs are a different story entirely."

"Do tell." She shot him an entertained look.

"Kids take apples to the teacher; puppy owners take the teacher to apple pie."

"I thought I liked my job. I was wrong—I love it!"

Ah, Vanessa, he thought, *if only a slice of apple pie could change how I felt about my life and job. There was a time when I had that same enthusiasm you have, but it's been gone for years now.*

❧

Vanessa fumbled for the telephone. It shrilled again, and she groaned as her fingers curled around the receiver and lifted it. "Hullo?"

"Vanessa?"

"Nathan?" She squinted at the neon orange numbers on her alarm clock—4:17? *This has to be a nightmare. It's not really happening.*

"Listen, I'm sorry to bother you—"

She shook herself. "Is it Jeff? Is something wrong?" In an instant, she was blazingly awake.

"No, but yes. Here's the deal: I just got an emergency call. The night watchman from the apartment complex I've started over on Beach and Tenth says it looks like the second story is buckling."

"Oh, no!"

"Jeff's class is going—"

"Whale watching today," she remembered aloud. Jeff had chattered about the trip every chance he got. He'd been looking forward to it for three weeks. "As I recall, you were supposed to go along."

"I'd ask Consuelo to go, but she gets seasick. I know Mondays are your day off, and I hate to ask. . ."

"Oh, I love whale watching! I'd be happy to go."

"Even with a class of six year olds?"

"The more, the merrier. I need to take Amber out on a boat, anyway."

"You're a lifesaver. I'll bundle up Jeff and be there in about twenty minutes."

"Don't bother. I'll come there."

Vanessa hung up the phone, hopped off the mattress, and flung the covers up in a hasty pretense of making the bed. Knowing the sea breeze would be stiff, she wore a T-shirt beneath a fleecy sweatshirt. Jeans, thick socks, and a battered pair of tennis shoes finished the outfit, then she dashed into the bathroom to grab her toothbrush.

Vanessa stopped dead in her tracks and burst out laughing. She'd fallen asleep, reading in bed, so she hadn't taken off what little makeup she normally wore. Mascara formed smoky rings around her eyes, a crease from her pillowcase looked like an earthquake fault line down her left cheek, and static electricity made every last strand of hair stick straight out in a bizarre impression of an atomic dandelion.

"Maybe I am having a nightmare, after all." She quickly scrubbed away the raccoon rings with a damp washcloth and brushed her teeth. Practically snatching herself bald due to the hairbrush getting caught in numerous tangles, Vanessa grumbled, "I'm going to have to talk to that man. He'll just have to understand he needs to arrange to have emergencies at a decent hour."

Amber woofed from beside her.

"Hey, don't stand up for the man. We girls are supposed to stick together." Vanessa grabbed a handful of essentials, zipped back into her bedroom, and recalled lending Val the big leather purse. Without it, she knew she had to make do.

Fifteen minutes later, she stood on the doorstep to Nathan's old saltbox in the predawn chill. She shivered and tapped quietly on the door. It opened almost instantly.

"Van, I can't thank you enough. I—what in the world?" He stared at the bulging pillowcase in her hands and gave her a baffled look.

Vanessa cruised past him and refused to look him in the eye. "I'm not trick-or-treating. If you dare say anything, you're dead meat. I told you I'm not a morning person."

"I didn't say a word."

She tried to act calm, cool, and collected as she pulled her windbreaker from the pillowcase. She should have put it on for the drive over, but she hadn't been functioning well enough to reason out that minor detail. Next, she withdrew Amber's leash and bright green jacket. A digital camera, a hairbrush, a tube of lip balm, a scrunchy for her hair, a visor, and a pair of sunglasses tumbled onto the coffee table as she upended the pillowcase.

Pretending to ignore Nathan's chuckle, she tossed the pillow onto the end of the couch, punched it a few times, toed out of her shoes, and flopped down. As she closed her eyes, she yawned.

Amber's paws pattered on the hardwood floor as she turned around in her customary triple circles before she plopped down directly next to the sofa. In contrast, Nathan's work boots sounded like a whole platoon of infantrymen as he approached. He detoured somewhere—but she refused to peek. All she wanted were twenty more winks. . .no, make that forty. A door latch popped open, then shut, and the infantry marched closer. "Here," Nathan growled softly. He covered Vanessa with a big, heavy blanket.

She didn't know where he'd gotten it from, and she didn't really care. As she snuggled a bit deeper into the cushions and blanket, she mumbled, "Better dig up an alarm clock for me."

"You won't need one. Jeff gets up at six-thirty on the dot."

"I'm not going to open my eyes, because if you're smiling at that revolting news, I'll have to crawl off the couch and leave."

"Thanks again, Van."

"G'night. G'bye."

The lock on the door clicked, and she dropped into a deep sleep filled with wild, disjointed dreams centering on talking puppies.

"I can't find my dad. Can you help me?"

"He's in the yard," she told the terrier.

"Thanks." The little pup trotted away. A door banged, and cold air washed over her as the little dog hollered, "Dad. Daaad! Where are you?"

Vanessa bolted from the couch. "Jeff!"

eleven

Vanessa stumbled over Amber and skidded through the kitchen. The clock on the stove read 6:33. She sped through the doorway in her stocking feet and ran out onto the wet lawn. "Jeff!"

Where was he? She nearly got whiplash, scanning the property. Red-and-blue plaid pajamas made him easy to spot once she turned toward the far end of the backyard. Both of his feet—bare feet—were on the rope ladder to his fort.

"I can't find Dad. I thought I'd climb up here. I can see better if—"

"Honey, your dad's not out here. He had a problem at work."

"But you told me he was in the yard." Jeff hung there and gave her a bewildered look.

"I must've been talking in my sleep. Come on back in the house."

Jeff jumped onto the grass and headed back toward the door. He turned and watched Amber and Lick both take care of business and pointed at them with shameless glee. "See what good puppies we have?"

"Terrific ones." She took a step. "Eww yuck! Your lawn is soaking wet!"

"Unh-huh. Dad made the timer on the sprinklers to go on early so the grass is dry for me to play on all day." Jeff trotted past her, into the house, with both dogs in his wake.

She squished after him. Once inside, she peeled off her socks and scowled at them. "What time does school start?"

"Eight."

"Great. I can toss these in the dryer." She mentally clicked off the minutes before they'd have to leave and felt a burst of relief that there was plenty of time for her to regain dry socks. At least there was one good thing about Jeff being an early riser—it gave a bit of space for solving odd predicaments that came up.

"Dad's gotta get home 'fore then, though. We're going on a field trip, and we've gotta be at the school early."

"Just how early?" She decided to break the news about being the substitute chaperon after she finished mopping up all of the wet foot and paw tracks on the linoleum.

"I dunno. It's on the paper." He banged his palm on the refrigerator door. The sheet of directions beneath his hand had a sketch of a whale in the upper right-hand corner.

"Thank You, Lord!" Vanessa snatched the page away from a pizza delivery magnet. She looked down at Jeff. "Know how I told you your dad had a great big problem at work? Well, since he figured he wouldn't get back in time, Amber and I are going to go with you instead."

"A dog can go to school?" Jeff's eyes got wider. "A dog wants to watch whales?"

"Isn't that cool?"

"Wow! Can I take Licorice too?"

"No, Sport. Amber's allowed to come along because when she grows up, she'll be a working dog. Give me a second here so I can get the scoop on what we're doing today."

" 'Kay."

Vanessa read the paper. The teacher had chosen a picture that depicted the kind of whale they'd most likely see—a point in her favor, and one she promptly lost when Vanessa spotted the second-to-the-last line, "Be sure to be here early! We're leaving at seven-thirty!"

Vanessa flipped the paper onto the kitchen counter and

glanced at the clock again. "We're on a tight schedule, Sport. We have to be at school in less than an hour. You'd better hurry up and get dressed."

Jeff rocketed up the stairs and reappeared five minutes later in an orange tank top and blue-and-purple-striped shorts. "I'm ready!"

"Only if you want to turn into a snowman. You'll freeze your toes off in that outfit. C'mon. Let's go find you something a bit warmer." Vanessa took his hand and climbed the stairs. She felt a little funny, wandering around the private part of Nathan's house.

What had to be the master bedroom was directly across from the landing. Early morning sunlight slanted through a beautiful, oval stained-glass window and splashed puddles of amber, rose, and blue over the rumpled, eggshell-colored sheets of a sleigh bed. In his rush, Nathan had dropped several coins that lay in a haphazard path from the antique oak dresser to the door.

It took but a second to take in that view, and Vanessa wanted to hurry on past it. Three doors gaped ahead. "Where's your bedroom?"

"Over here." Jeff tugged her past a bathroom where the towels hung askew, into what still looked like a nursery. The wallpaper featured pastel zoo animals, yellow gingham curtains dressed the window, and a baby blue, three-drawer dresser stood against the far wall. All three drawers were ajar.

"Boy, you really were in a hurry," Vanessa said as she took in the garments spilling from each drawer. "How about if you find a pair of jeans, and I'll come up with a shirt?"

" 'Kay."

Vanessa straightened out the drawers as swiftly as she could while trying to be unobtrusive. She pretended to consider different shirts before settling on an undershirt and a bright yellow sweatshirt that would make him easy to spot in a crowd. She made his bed and set the clothes on it with a pat. "You change while I see about some breakfast."

"It's Monday," he said as though that fact had special significance.

"What does that have to do with breakfast?"

"Waffles and orange juice! We always have them on Monday." He even nodded as if to assert it was the routine every decent home ought to follow.

Once Vanessa reached the kitchen, she glanced at all of the cupboards and cabinets. Where does Nathan keep the waffle iron? She could wait a few minutes 'til Jeff came down to answer that question. In the meantime, since there wasn't a carton of orange juice in the refrigerator, she opened the freezer. There, in the door, just next to the can of orange juice, sat a box of toaster waffles.

"Quick and easy." She grabbed both items and spun around toward the counter. It struck her as odd that Nathan bought juice that had to be prepared and waffles that were premade, but then again, he probably grabbed them during a dash through the frozen-food section.

Jeff plunked down the stairs, and they sat at the table and ate while the puppies chomped on kibble. Jeff banged the heels of his tennis shoes on the rungs of his chair. "What did you make for lunch?"

Lunch! Oh, great. How could I forget about that? She gave him an I've-got-this-covered look. "We're a team. We're making lunch together."

He dawdled over a second waffle as she wiped down the toaster and put it away. Mouth full, he pointed at a cabinet. "We gots granola bars and fruit rollies up there."

It didn't take long to slap together a decent lunch. They brushed their teeth, and then Vanessa groaned, "I forgot to put my socks in the dryer!"

"You can wear some of mine."

"Thanks, but my feet are a bit bigger than yours."

He opened the dryer and fished out a crew sock with two black stripes at the top and another with no color striping but gray patches at the toe and heel. "Here. You can wear Dad's. We aren't gonna be late, are we? Teacher said if we're late, the bus will leave without us."

Vanessa yanked on the mismatched socks, ignored the fact that the heels poked out at ankle level, and shoved her feet into her tennis shoes. "You put Lick in the backyard. I'll grab my stuff, and we'll be outta here."

"Are you sure Dad won't come with us? The three of us always have fun together."

"Yeah, we do manage to have fun together, but if your dad woke me up early for anything other than an emergency, I'd dump him right off the boat."

She gathered all of the gear, snapped the leash and jacket on Amber, and they raced out the door. Jeff's school was a brisk half-mile walk, and they chattered the whole way there. The minute they reached the edge of the school grounds, Vanessa spied a tall, dark, handsome man leaning against a cinder-block wall. "Nathan!"

☙

Nathan strove to look casual, but it wasn't easy. Luckily, Jeff gave him a moment of diversion.

"Dad! You're here! You'd better be careful. 'Nessa said she'd dump you over the side of the boat if you showed up."

Vanessa's pink cheeks tattled that she hadn't counted on that little quip getting repeated. Nathan chuckled at her. "Gotta watch what you say around Jeff. He's got a knack for remembering the smallest things and repeating them at the most inopportune moment."

"So I noticed." She shrugged. "I deserved that. I ought to think before I speak, but that's a real weak point for me. I take it the apartment emergency isn't a massive crisis after all?"

"Yes and no. The watchman thought the second floor was buckling. It isn't. We designed it so the upstairs of the deluxe apartments will have either sunken baths or a raised platform for the bed and a lower conversation or play area."

"I see."

Nathan thought of how tired she'd been when she'd dragged herself to his front door earlier that morning. He quickly added, "But while I was there, I looked at the ceiling beams for the main entrance and noticed they're already warped a little. They'll continue to twist until they torque the supports and weaken the vaulted ceilings. I had to track down the manufacturer back East and read him the riot act. He's sending replacements on the train today. It's going to set us behind schedule a full three days. If I hadn't caught that, it would have been a real embarrassment."

"Doing quality work matters to you."

"Yes, it does." He raised his brows. "Am I forgiven, or are you planning to go through with that plot to dump me overboard and feed me to the whales?"

"There's nothing to forgive. Jeff and I had a fun morning. He's a great helper."

"Yeah, I fed the puppies and got Van some of your socks." Jeff giggled. "Hers got wet."

Nathan gave Vanessa a stricken look. "Lick didn't. . .um—"

"No! Oh, no, he didn't. I tromped out in the backyard on your just-watered lawn."

"Ah. Gotcha. One of the hazards of having a puppy."

"Nope. She didn't come out to get the puppies; she came out to get me!"

"Sport, what were you doing out in the backyard?"

"Vanessa said you were out there." Jeff tugged on Nathan's belt and stood up on tiptoe. In a stage whisper, he added, "Dad, she talks in her sleep!"

With a mock look of exasperation, Vanessa propped her hands on her hips and tapped her toe on the sidewalk. "And you, Jeffrey Adams, talk waaay too much while you're awake!"

"Yep!" Jeff giggled at her theatrics. With a gleeful look, he added, "Dad, guess what? Your socks are too big on her. Waaay too big."

"No kidding. Your dad's feet are huge." She pinched her jeans just above the knees and hiked them up several inches. "Have you ever seen anything so ridiculous?"

Nathan tilted back his head and roared.

"Listen, Mister, it's not that funny!"

"Oh, yes, it is." He couldn't stop chuckling. "Let me guess. Jeff got those out of the dryer."

"How did you know?" Vanessa and Jeff both asked him.

Nathan copied Vanessa's action. He hiked up his own jeans and displayed a plain sock and a striped one. "I was in such a hurry to get out of the house this morning, I grabbed whatever was handy. I'm wearing the matching set!"

The look on Vanessa's face was priceless. She blinked, her face split into a huge grin, and giggles spilled out of her. When she finally calmed down, she announced, "It looks like you have everything well in hand. They don't need me as an extra chaperon, so I'm taking your funny socks and going home."

Nathan dared to reach over and grab her hand. "Actually, we do need you. When I got here, Miss Sanderly was having a conniption fit. It seems one of the mothers who offered to accompany us woke up with a toothache."

"You'll come, Vanessa, won't you? Pleeeze?" Jeff jigged at her side.

"Of course she is. She wouldn't miss this trip for anything."

Nathan didn't want to give her an opportunity to back out. He knew he ought to feel guilty about roping her into this; the truth of it was, he didn't feel anything other than pure anticipation.

twelve

"Val, you wouldn't have believed it," Vanessa told her sister as they met at church for the midweek service. "One of the other kids on the field trip didn't have a jacket. Nathan grabbed one out of the jump seat of his truck and gave it to the little boy."

"That's good. Remember the time we went whale watching and nearly froze?"

"Yes, but I thought we were done, and it turned out that was just the beginning."

"Oh?"

"They could live out of that truck for a week. No exaggeration—they have so much stuff all organized in the cab, NASA ought to ask for packing tips. Nathan started rummaging for food so he'd have a lunch to take."

"Well, we have energy bars and water in our cars."

Vanessa shook her head. "But we don't have cheese-and-crackers snack packs. A juice box."

"Sis, Jeff's a little kid. Nathan's got to keep munchies for him."

"If it stopped there, I wouldn't think a thing of it. Then he started pulling stuff out in earnest. Beef jerky. Dried apricots. A little can of peanuts. Granola bars. Those individual cups of applesauce and plastic spoons!"

Valene's eyes grew huge. "The man even had spoons?"

Muting her voice since they were entering the sanctuary, Vanessa said, "Yes. Spoons. And paper towels. Nathan packed a better lunch than I did!"

To her credit, Val muffled her laughter. As they slid into the pew, she wondered aloud, "Had he just gone grocery shopping or something?"

"No." Vanessa plunked her purse down and muttered, "He keeps earthquake supplies in his truck and car." She gave her sister a daffy look. "To top it all off, we cruised all day and didn't see a single whale."

"That's too bad."

"Jeff was so disappointed."

The music started, so their conversation ended abruptly. Vanessa stared at the back of the pew in front of her and let out a silent sigh. She'd struggled to get Jeff ready, lunches made, and the two of them to school on time; Nathan did it every single school day, and he managed it quite well. He operated on a smooth, near-perfect level, and she could be the poster girl for Insecurities Anonymous—well, she would be if they had anything more than a friendship. *But we don't. We're just pals.* That realization flooded her with an odd sense of relief. *Yeah. It's good Nathan is so good at handling things on his own. Sure it is. It works out well for him and Jeff.*

She continued to think of them until Kip slid into the pew and somehow managed to bump Val over so he sat between them. Once the service got underway, Pastor MacIntosh made announcements. After he mentioned one particular upcoming activity, Vanessa and Valene both leaned forward to make eye contact and exchanged a meaningful look.

❧

"He'd have such a good time."

Nathan stared out of the dugout, not wanting to look at Vanessa's pleading face. Kip sent a ball sailing into center field and made it to second base while folks cheered. Nathan hoped Van would get involved in the game and drop the subject.

"I'm working, but you can go with him, Nathan. If you're already busy, plenty of the parents are going, and they'd keep close watch on Jeff."

He didn't respond.

The shortstop caught a fly, and Kip got tagged out on third. Nathan bolted off the bench, eager to get out on the field, away from the conversation.

Vanessa halted him. "I'm sorry, Nathan. I didn't mean to pressure you. I promised I wouldn't invite you to church—I didn't stop to think you'd consider a primary department outing would fall under that heading. I knew Jeff would enjoy going to the tide pools, and well—" She let out a gusty sigh. "I understand. It's with the church's primary department. I can see now it was a mistake for me to say anything."

Tears glossed her eyes. Nathan drew in a quick breath. Part of him caved in; the other part rebelled. She wasn't just a do-gooder, trying to involve his son in church—she really cared about Jeff. *But I'm not getting sucked into all of this church stuff.*

"I really blew it, didn't I?"

"Vanessa, let's just drop it for now and play ball."

"All right." She paused and added, "I'll drop it." As he began to walk off, he heard her mutter, "For now."

In the last inning, Nathan channeled all of his churning emotions into his swing. His grand slam bought the Altar Egos's triumph. As he ran the bases and touched home plate, the team and crowd went wild. Only he knew deep inside, the last thing he felt was victorious.

❧

Saturday, after the puppy kindergarten class, Nathan curled his hand around Vanessa's arm. Shock jolted through her at the intensity of his gaze.

"Can you give me a minute?"

"Um, yeah. Sure. What is it, Nathan?"

"Saturday mornings aren't working out well for me." He let go of her. "The next few weeks will be impossible. Can you work with Jeff and me on training Lick on a catch-as-catch-can basis?"

A sick feeling churned in her stomach. She'd pressured him about the tide-pool trip for Jeff, and this seemed like a polite version of "So long, see ya later."

Lord, I'm so sorry. I need to learn to be patient. I acted in haste, and I've pushed him away from You.

Nathan tugged on Lick's leash to pull him back from sniffing at a patch of grass. Nathan kept his gaze trained downward. "Jeff really wants to go to the tide pools next Saturday. I can't be in two places at once."

"He'll love it! Be sure to take your camera and get pictures."

Nathan looked up, and the sparkle in his eye warmed her heart. He wasn't trying to bail out or to mollify her—she could see that he really wanted to go.

"It's been so long since I dug out the camera. Evie always took snapshots. I just haven't had the heart. When you took your camera whale watching, I got an attack of the guilts."

When he mentioned his wife, the sparkle in his eyes dimmed, and it made Vanessa want to comfort him. She sensed he'd not welcome anything overt, so instead, she went for simple reassurance. "Not that I got any great photos, anyway. We didn't see a single whale."

Nathan shrugged. "Since he didn't get to see any whales, I thought you were right—he ought to get a chance to see sea creatures somehow."

Vanessa nodded. If she said something right now, she'd probably make an utter fool of herself, either hugging him or blubbering for joy.

"It's not just next Saturday. If it were a matter of missing a single class, we'd probably be able to catch on and catch up. It's more complicated than that. The following Saturday, I'll be out of town, and the week after, I have an appointment with a client. Lick's just too knot-headed for me to believe we can miss three sessions in a row and train him to be obedient."

"I'm sure we can work out a few private training sessions."

"Great. If we can get him to behave, I'll be a happy camper. I don't expect him to ever be a model citizen like Amber."

"When we're through with him, he will be. It just takes patience. With patience, you can do just about anything."

❧

Late that evening, Vanessa pulled a diskette out of her computer. *Lord, I just wanna say something here. I know I told Nathan all it took was patience to get things done. I did qualify it with a 'just about.' Well, I've been trying to make the accounts balance, and they won't. I can't. This doesn't just take patience—it's going to take a miracle!*

She grimaced at the memory of her sage words, then turned that grimace toward the shoebox full of receipts. Practice—she practiced plenty of things, but patience wasn't one of them. That commodity just hit an all-time low.

In sheer desperation, she filled a bag with gourmet doggy treats and hit the road. She tromped into Val's condo and cried, "I'm throwing myself on your mercy. I even brought bribes for Hero."

"It's the end of the month." Val arched a brow. "Let me guess: You can't get the books to balance."

"Bingo."

"Hero will be happy to have the treats. I, on the other hand, refuse to be bribed."

"Val, come on. I'm dying here."

"So am I. Here's the deal: You give Hero the rest of his

puppy shots. I can't stand to do it myself, and Dr. Bainbridge's office is only open during the hours I work."

"I'm more than willing to do that. You've got a deal." Vanessa poured herself a cup of tea. "Then again, I would have been willing to do it for you anyway."

Val laughed. "I know. Just like I would have straightened out your record keeping for you anyway."

While Val clicked around on the computer and resolved all the quirks and misfiled information on Vanessa's ledger, Van dug through the cabinets and found a vase.

"What're you up to now?"

"Don't pay any attention to me. Just crunch the numbers." Vanessa pulled a variety of silk flowers from her athletic bag and put together an arrangement for Val's living room.

"All done," Val said.

"Me too. Take a look."

Val walked into the living room, and her face lit up. "That's perfect! I don't know how you do that kind of stuff. Arts and crafts are my waterloo."

"Yeah, well, you got the smarts; I got the crafts. Believe me, if I had to pick, I would have taken the brains."

"You do have brains," Val protested. She then grimaced. "But I'm worried you're not using them. We need to have a talk."

"Now what did I do?" Van turned sideways on the couch and watched as her twin searched for the right words. *Uh-oh. Whatever this is, it's a biggie....*

Val paced across the floor and turned back. "I think you need to draw a definite line with Nathan."

"Draw a line?"

"He's not a believer. Well, he is, but he's not living his faith. He's bitter toward the Lord, and that's not the kind of man you ought to be dating."

Vanessa snorted. "Dating? You've gotta be kidding me. We have his son and two dogs everywhere we go. It's nothing romantic at all."

"Just because it starts off innocently doesn't mean it'll stay that way." Valene sat down and curled her hand around Vanessa's wrist. "You'd be wise to spend less time with him and more time with a man who is practicing a strong daily walk with Christ."

"We're not dating, Val, and Nathan will eventually restore his relationship with the Lord. Christ didn't turn his back on those who strayed. He said as a shepherd He'd search for every lost lamb. If all I ever do is hang out with Christians who have no doubts or questions, who's going to reach out to those who are out of relationship or hurting? That wouldn't be living my faith."

"You have a point, but I'm trying to make you see the difference between being casual friends and losing your heart. Nathan is handsome, well-to-do, and kind."

"I have several guy friends who are handsome or well-off, and they're all good-hearted. They're just friends."

"But how many of them would have called you at four in the morning to pinch-hit for their kid's field trip. Why did Nathan call you?"

"Let's see. For starters, my other friends don't have kids. As for Nathan, it was a Monday. Most people work on Mondays, but it's my day off. Nathan knows I love the ocean. Jeff and I are buddies. Besides—it's good for Amber to go on all different modes of transportation, and she hadn't been on a boat yet."

Val gave her an I'm-not-buying-your-story look.

"Get this: One of the kids came up to us and asked Jeff, 'Is she your dad's girlfriend?' and I said, 'Nope. Amber is my dog, not his.' See? I made it clear I'm not romantically entangled."

Val laid her head on the back of the couch and groaned. "Why did I have to be right? I just told you, you have brains, but you're not using them. This is going to be a disaster."

"Let's see." Vanessa ticked off points on her hand. "Jeff learned a lesson about integrity. I sold a dog. I'm even earning money on training." She wiggled those three fingers in the air. "If that isn't enough, look at the more important issues: Nathan is now playing ball with the church team, and he's renewed his friendship with Kip. Jeff is going to the tide pools with the primary department—and Nathan is taking him!"

All five fingers stuck up in the air. She then tightened them together to form a scoop, turned her hand palm up, and lifted it toward heaven. "It's really not in my hands at all, Val. It's in God's."

thirteen

Once or twice a week, Nathan managed to find a time slot that Vanessa had free. They met at the park across from her shop and worked with Lick's training. Sometimes Jeff stayed at home with Consuelo. Other times he was at a birthday party or at a friend's house. About half the time, he came along and enjoyed learning too.

Nathan liked how Van paid attention to Jeff and never acted like he was a tagalong. The two of them often traded silly jokes and romped, yet she still earned and held his respect.

If they did puppy training in his backyard, she made a habit of bringing a snack of some variety and insisting that they all wedge into the fort to share it. Having deduced that he was all thumbs in the kitchen, she frequently managed to bring something she'd baked—cream puffs, cookies shaped like dog biscuits, apple tarts, or cupcakes with cherries made of gumdrops decorating the top.

Two adults, one wiggly boy, and two puppies in the fort's tight space always turned out to be the highlight of the day—and not because of the food. Nathan could sit close to Vanessa, relish her sunny laugh, try to determine what odd combination of fragrances she'd put together, and swipe a nibble from her fingertips.

Whenever he and Vanessa met without Jeff, Nathan tried to find ways to prolong their time together. They'd eaten at several fast-food places that featured outdoor picnic tables so the dogs wouldn't have to be left in the car—something neither he nor Vanessa would consider. It didn't exactly qualify as the most romantic way to edge into a relationship, but he didn't care. Just being with Vanessa made his day.

One hitch bothered him. When they ate, she prayed. He knew the Lord was an integral part of her life. She'd mention things about a program at church or occasionally quote something he knew came from Psalms or Proverbs. If anything, he sensed she made a concerted effort not to swamp him with religious stuff.

He appreciated her restraint. It made him uncomfortable when folks got all churchy around him. Nathan knew it was guilt. He flatly refused to explore that emotion. God took Evie away. How could God ask for a man's soul when He robbed him of his heart?

Over time, he'd begun to feel less awkward when Vanessa would say a simple, quick grace. He'd turned down a few invitations to church by a couple of the guys on the team until Vanessa had grabbed the bull by the horns. After practice one evening, she'd faced the whole team and announced, "Nathan knows he has a standing invitation to church. I promised him I wouldn't wheedle or plot so he'd get roped into attending. When he's ready, he'll come. Until then, let's leave it be." Integrity. She had it in spades.

What kind of man was he, to want to court a woman who walked so closely with the Lord? He knew all about being in step with the Lord. He'd been that way once upon a time, and he'd willingly worn the mantle of the spiritual head of his home with an awareness of its responsibilities and blessings. His marriage with Evie blossomed under God's grace and leading—until Evie died, when simple faith suddenly wasn't enough. Vanessa deserved a man of faith. *But I can't let her go. What kind of man does that make me?*

❧

"Dad, that was so much fun! Can we go again? Please?"

Nathan looked down at Jeff's sun-kissed cheeks and silently agreed. They'd had a terrific day down at the tide pools. The group got there just as the tide went out, and the pocked rock formations held countless wonders. Children darted from one pool to the next, shrieking with joy. They'd squat next to a little hollowed-out retreat and point at darting, tiny fish or touch limpets. *Yeah, I could go for a day like that again. It was relaxing, fun. . . .*

"Please, Dad. I wanna go back there."

"I had a great time too. Maybe we could do it again. What would you think about taking Vanessa and Amber with us?"

"That'd be super-duper! Let's go tomorrow."

"Sorry, Sport." He lifted the blankets, and Jeff tumbled into bed. Covering his son, Nathan said, "Tomorrow's Sunday. Van works in the afternoon after she goes to church. The animals have to be fed and watered."

"But we could go in the morning!"

Nathan shook his head. "Van goes to church."

"Dad? Why don't we go to church? I gots lots of friends who go to Van's church. We're all good buddies."

"Church isn't just supposed to be about who you go to see."

"Then what is it about? I know!" Jeff popped up and gave Nathan an earnest look. "It's 'bout God and Jesus and stuff— like in the songs the kids were singing today, huh?"

"Yeah." Nathan tucked him back in, ruffled his hair, and kissed his forehead. "Enough talk. Go to sleep." Before Jeff could pursue the conversation, he left the room.

❧

"I'm going for the fives." Dad set aside two of the dice and dropped the other three back in the cup. They made a hollow, rattling sound before he dumped them out again. They tumbled across the flower-patterned vinyl tablecloth and came to rest a few inches past a small crease that acted as a speed bump.

Vanessa leaned back in the molded plastic patio chair and relished the night breeze off the sea. It rustled through the mulberry tree in the corner of the backyard. She laughed. "Remember that year Val and I did the silk project?"

"Fourth grade," her mother recalled. "Those silkworms you raised were disgusting."

"Now I thought they were interesting, Mom." Dad set aside another five and plunked the last two dice into his cup. "The teacher said our Van was the only kid she ever had who actually kept them alive and spinning."

"Because we had the mulberry leaves. It wasn't hard at all—I just picked a few leaves and dumped them in each morning. We got a good grade on the project because of Val. She wrote a great paper to go along with it."

"And your illustrations were amazing," Mom added.

Dad sent the dice across the table and bellowed gleefully, "Yahtzee!"

"Can you believe that? The last roll of the game, and Dad gets a Yahtzee!"

As they put away the game, Mom asked, "What made you think of the silkworms?"

"The mulberry tree."

Dad took another sip of his tea. "It's a good source of shade, but the berries sure make a mess. Every year, I say something about taking it out and putting in something that won't be such a hassle, but Mom won't let me."

"Why not?"

"She's sentimental. You used to hold your animal hospitals under it."

Vanessa grinned at the memory. "It's amazing you didn't

go broke, buying me gauze and tape for all of those bandages I made."

"What's amazing is, all of those animals just sat there and let you mummy wrap them!" Mom laughed. "Dad's just as sentimental as I am. He sticks nails into the ground by the hydrangea so the flower petals will turn pretty colors. Remember how you and Val used to play "Wedding" and use those poufy flower balls as your bridal bouquets?"

"And the yellow chenille pipe cleaner rings!" Vanessa looked over at the hydrangea, then back at her parents. "We had a storybook childhood."

Dad cleared his throat. "Speaking of weddings. . ."

"Is someone getting married?"

"We're talking about you, Sweetheart." Mom scooted her chair closer. "You're spending an awful lot of time with that Adams man."

"Did Val put you up to this?"

"Nope." Dad leaned on the table and shook his head. "Honey, we reared you to do the right thing, to live by the Bible. You know you're not to set your heart on a man who isn't walking with the Lord. My understanding is Nathan Adams lost his wife, and he's bitter toward God."

"He is."

"Then why are you dating him?" Mom frowned.

Vanessa sighed. "Once and for all, we are not dating. I get paid each time we meet, and you certainly didn't rear me to be that kind of woman!"

Her mom's eyes widened, and she chided, "Vanessa!"

"Okay, Mom. Sorry. I got a bit carried away, but all of this concern feels like such an overreaction." When her parents didn't respond, she hastened on. "I'm giving him puppy obedience lessons. Most of the time, we have Amber, his black Lab, and his son with us. We've never eaten out unless you count an ice cream cone or fast food. He's a friend."

"Friends can become more than friends"—Mom looked her in the eye—"especially when the woman is as compassionate and sympathetic as you are. Your whole childhood, you gravitated toward people and animals who needed special attention. You've grown into an empathetic woman who cares freely and deeply. I'm worried that you're getting absorbed into Nathan Adams's world. He's a wounded man, and you can't fix him."

Vanessa rubbed her face with both hands and looked away for a moment, then looked back at her mother. Quietly, she admitted, "I know I can't. I'm just trying to come alongside him as a Christian sister."

Mom dipped her head ever so slightly and looked at Vanessa with her I-mean-business glare. "Sister? Friend? Those are nice labels, but my radar is sending off boyfriend alarms."

"Mom, I'm not dating him. I'm so busy with the shop and the private lessons and the baseball team and the puppy training club, there isn't time. My life is full, and my heart isn't empty. I figure God will put the right man in my life when He wills it."

"Nathan is on that team, isn't he?" Dad asked pointedly.

"Yes, he is." Vanessa grinned. "And he just took his son to the tide pools with the primary department today. I have faith that the Good Shepherd will bring back His straying lamb. It's a matter of letting God be God."

"Don't get involved romantically with a man and expect him to change." Dad stood. "It's wrong, Honey."

"I agree, Dad. I need to get going. I'll see you at church tomorrow."

ಶಿ

Nathan lay in bed and stared at the stained-glass window. A streetlight shone through it just enough to make the pattern apparent. Evie had surprised him with the window the year she was carrying Jeff. It was a Christmas present, and she'd managed to save up the money for it by squirreling away her change. He'd been so surprised. *Little things add up. Just think—we're going to have the best little thing of all.* She'd wear that dreamy look and rub her tummy.

Then, too, once he set the window into their bedroom wall, she'd lie next to him and imagine all the different things the window could mean. *Three flowers. . .you, me, and the baby. Or is it the Trinity? Father, Son, and Holy Spirit. . .the ribbon holding them is love. I'm sure of that. Nothing is stronger than love.*

Now, he lay there, and her words echoed in his mind. So did Jeff's. *Dad? Why don't we go to church?*

He rolled over and smacked his pillow.

God, You know why I don't go to church. I refuse to be a hypocrite. I'm not going to go and pretend I understand. I don't. I don't have the kind of faith that makes everything okay and lets me dump everything into Your hands. I'm mad. No, I'm livid. Bad enough, You took my wife, but how could You rob Jeff of his mother? I wouldn't want someone who held a grudge against me in my home. Why should I go to Yours?

Sleep wouldn't come. Hearing a light, puppy whimper, Nathan shoved aside his blankets and got up. He took Lick out to the backyard and grumbled, "Okay. Do your business."

How many times had he heard Vanessa give Amber that same command? He'd chuckled the first time he overheard it. That was back when he didn't know the special commands she used in training. Now it all made sense and came as second nature.

Lick complied, then ran to the other side of the yard. "Come." Nathan waited, but the puppy ignored him.

He squatted down and reached out. "Come, Lick."

The puppy continued to wander on his own path.

"Lick, come on, Boy."

Lick perked up his head, his tail wagged, and he bounded across the yard, straight to Nathan.

Nathan felt a spurt of irritation, then squelched it. He couldn't punish this silly little, wiggly ball of fluff. Lick had obeyed the call and come. If he got punished, he'd be less likely to come again in the future. Instead, Nathan cradled the puppy in his arms and took him inside. As he stuck Lick back in his bed in the corner of Jeff's room, Jeff stirred.

"Dad?"

"What?"

"You never answered my question. Can we go to church?"

Nathan stayed motionless and stared across the dim room at his innocent little boy. *I don't have to make a big deal of this. We'll go just once. That'll satisfy him.* Even that agreement felt like a huge concession.

"I wanna go."

Each word strained his vocal cords as Nathan said, "We'll go tomorrow."

fourteen

His shoes pinched. His dress socks had a hole in one toe, courtesy of Licorice. One of the buttons on his suit dangled by a thread, and he'd forgotten he'd tossed his favorite tie in the drawer the last time he wore it, so he had to settle for another one that had a small mustard stain. For being a successful businessman, he looked like a bum.

Man looks at the outward appearance, but the Lord looks at the heart. The verse ran through his mind, and as Nathan pulled into a parking space, he muttered, "I'm striking out on both accounts."

Giggling, Jeff bounced along the sidewalk as they headed toward the sanctuary. "Hey—there's Andy! He's in my class at school."

It didn't take much time to settle Jeff into a Sunday-school class, then Nathan stared at the sanctuary. Each step took resolve. *I could just leave and come back to pick up Jeff, but I said we'd go to church. If I don't stay, I would be lying.*

He hadn't attended Seaside Chapel before and was surprised to discover how that very fact actually made it easier to go inside the sanctuary. Instead of having to endure the inevitable flood of memories from Mercy Springs, there was simple curiosity on his part. A greeter shook his hand, and an usher handed him the bulletin—familiar rituals that should have given comfort, but just left him feeling hollow. He could endure one day of this.

He saw Valene sitting near the aisle. Amber was lying curled up, "being small," just to the side of the pew. A couple sat beside Val—her parents, he presumed. Nathan slipped into the pew directly behind her, set down the bulletin, and leaned forward. Tapping her on the shoulder, he murmured, "Don't look now—the roof might cave in. I came to church."

"You'd better look," she whispered back. "I'm Val."

"I know." He flashed a quick smile at her. "Van couldn't sit as still as you do or stay quiet. She'd be chattering up a storm with half the congregation and make a last-minute mad dash for a seat." He glanced around, hoping to see Vanessa. With Amber right here, she had to be close—a fact that made him feel a little less anxious. Until now, he hadn't realized how much he was counting on her being there to be his lifeline. "Where is your sister?"

"Van's singing in the choir today. Amber's supposed to stay here, but I'm keeping an eye on her."

"She looks a lot more comfortable than I feel." He couldn't believe he'd blurted that out.

She gave him a timid smile. "I'm glad you came. Have you met our parents, Ellen and Bill?"

"No." He stood and shook Ellen's and Bill's hands. "You have wonderful daughters."

"Thank you. We hear you have a terrific little boy," Ellen said.

"And a powerhouse swing," Bill added. "The team's finally winning a few games this year."

"Why don't you come up and sit with us?" Ellen invited.

Just then, another family entered from the side and filed right in next to the Zobels. Nathan grinned. "Thanks, but I'm fine." He took a seat and pretended to study the bulletin.

Nathan figured it served him right that he assumed Vanessa would be waiting to sit next to him. She probably served on a few committees and substitute taught a Sunday-school class too. He'd never met anyone with her vitality. If something needed doing, she'd be in the middle of it.

Valene and her parents were gracious, but it just wasn't the same. He knew Van and Val were identical, but the odd thing was, he really never gave Val a second thought. Vanessa kindled something inside of him, and beside her, all other women paled to insignificance.

Shy Valene sat in front of him and dipped her head as she meditated before the service began. He'd noticed Vanessa tended to turn her face toward heaven when she prayed. She acted just as open with the Father as she did with people.

How can she trust the Lord and rely on Him so completely? Innocence? Is it just that she hasn't been burned by life yet? God let loose a nuclear bomb in my life. Nothing's left of my soul but a charred shell. I believe in Him, but how can I ever trust Him again?

He didn't have much time for reflection. The worship leader got up to the microphone and welcomed everyone. He directed them to all stand and greet someone. A couple of the guys from the baseball team came over and shook his hand.

Part of Nathan liked already knowing some of the folks— it made it seem a little less foreign. On the other hand, he felt trapped. Just because he came this once, he didn't want them to all start bugging him to show up again.

While his attention was diverted, the choir filed in. Nathan looked up and spotted Vanessa at once. She perked up and smiled at him. *Best welcome I got. . .* Close on the warmth of that feeling, his common sense kicked in. *But this is just a onetime deal.*

The pianist played a couple chords, and the choir started in. Soon, the music director had the whole congregation singing.

Funny thing, hymns. They're classics. Never paid attention, but they can be welcoming and comforting—probably the familiarity of them. Odd, after five years, I remember almost all of the words. Two of the worship songs were new—he didn't know the tunes, but that forced him to attend to the lyrics more closely. All in all, the music time didn't feel too awkward.

Nathan followed the music minister's directions to stand and sit when everyone else did. He took his seat again as an elderly couple tottered from the front row of the choir to the microphone and started to sing, "It Is Well with My Soul." Clearly, their hearts were in the right place, but their vocal cords weren't. Nathan never pretended to have a whole lot of talent in the music department, but even he knew they were each singing in completely different keys. To make matters worse, one of them wore a hearing aid that managed to buzz off and on. The microphone picked up the high-pitched tone and turned it into a shrill siren.

Amber stood up, right there in the center of the main aisle and started to "sing" along in howl.

"Hush!" Valene tried to silence Amber, but Amber wagged her head from side to side almost as if she were saying no. She tilted her head back and continued to howl.

Nathan glanced up at the choir and saw Vanessa's incredulous expression. Valene glowed bright red in embarrassment as she continued to whisper very softly, "Hush, Amber. That's enough."

Having spent a lot of time with them, Nathan remembered the command Vanessa used on the rare occasions when Amber needed correction. He leaned forward and used her tactic. In a firm voice, pitched low enough to mean business, yet not so loud as to travel through the entire sanctuary, he said, "That's enough."

Immediately, Amber went quiet.

"Down," Nathan commanded.

Amber backed up a few steps, lay down, and rested her

chin on the edge of his pew. Nathan glanced up at the choir, and Vanessa mouthed, "Thank you."

Fortunately the man in charge of the sound system managed to adjust the microphone so the duet finished without any further technical or canine embellishment. Nathan knew he'd never forget that hymn.

After the benediction, Bill Zobel turned around. "I have a hankering for Chinese. Why don't you collect your son and meet us all at the Paper Lantern?"

"Only if he'll promise to order something with some zing," Vanessa declared as she walked up. "My parents and Val all have sissy mouths. I'm tired of sharing bland stuff."

"The hotter, the better." Nathan grinned. "But Jeff is going to be a traitor. He always wants something sweet like orange chicken."

"My favorite!" Ellen smiled.

"See?" Vanessa groaned.

"I'll order hot-and-spicy Hunan beef if you get firecracker shrimp or kung pao chicken." He got a kick out of seeing how Vanessa perked up. The woman was so bright, she could masquerade as a thousand-watt lightbulb.

Val wrinkled her nose. "I'll order beds for both of you at Community General after you burn holes in your stomachs with that stuff."

Nathan shrugged. "If my cooking hasn't sent me to the hospital, nothing will."

ىگ

"Dad, what is the duck peeking at?"

"Peking used to be a place in China, but they changed what it's called to Beijing," Van explained as Nathan gave his son a baffled look. "The people at that table across from us want to try a dish that is named after the city."

"Oh. So those people wanna eat funny stuff." Jeff leaned

closer to Vanessa. "Did you hear them? They're getting mushy pork."

"Mu shu pork sounds good to me." Vanessa's dad closed the menu. He grinned at Jeff. "It's sort of like skinny pancakes they fill with pork. They're good. I'll get that, and we can try it together."

"My dog eats pancakes. My dog and Valene's dog are brothers. I wish I had a brother."

The muscle in Nathan's cheek twitched. His eyes narrowed for a split second. He took a long, deep breath, and his features smoothed. Poking his forefinger into Jeff's ribs, he rumbled, "Oh, no. You're enough for me. Between you and Lick, I've got my hands full."

Jeff giggled and squirmed. "Lick got one of Dad's socks today. He ran all over the house with it in his mouth."

Nathan looked into Vanessa's eyes. She felt her pulse speed up a bit. "See what kind of trainer you are? You swiped my socks, so now the dog's doing it too."

"His socks?" her mother echoed. "You swiped his socks?"

Shaking his head, Jeff blabbed, "She wore Dad's socks. Dad and Van both had one with stripes and one that didn't have stripes. They matched each other."

Mom about spilled the tea she was pouring into Dad's cup as she croaked, "How did you end up wearing his socks?"

"Vanessa talks in her sleep." Jeff wiggled with delight. "She told me—"

Uh-oh. This is unbelievable. Damage-control time here. "Nathan had an emergency. At work. I went over—to his house, not to his work. He called me." She knew she was babbling, but she couldn't help herself. "Early in the morning—"

"Vanessa bailed me out of a tight spot. About a week ago, I had to dash off to a construction site, so she baby-sat Jeff for me." Nathan finished the explanation smoothly. It didn't escape her notice that he made it abundantly clear he hadn't stayed in the house with her there.

Whew.

"You ready to order?" The waitress held her pen poised over an abused pad of paper.

"Mom?" Dad prompted.

"I heard Jeff likes orange chicken, so I'd better order something different so we'll have an assortment. I'll go for some sweet-and-sour ribs."

"I'd like the mushroom chicken, please." Val snapped the menu shut.

"Mu shu pork," Dad added.

Jeff got up on his knees and leaned across the table. "Are those our pancakes?"

"You better believe it!"

"Goody!"

Jeff managed to give them all a rundown of his Sunday school lesson. The whole time he spoke, Nathan kept his arm around his son's shoulders, but with his free hand, he pensively turned his teacup in slow, exacting clockwise clicks.

What is he thinking?

When the food came, Jeff changed topics. "Looky, Dad! Looky! That thing in the middle of the table is a merry-go-round!"

"It's called a lazy Susan. We'll all put our food on there and spin it around so anyone who wants to can have a taste. Pretty nifty, huh, Sport?"

"Can you put one in our table? It's cool!" He turned to Vanessa. "My dad can do anything. He can make anything!"

She thought of the beautiful, old oak pedestal table she'd seen at Nathan's house. "Your table is round like this one, but I think it would look kind of strange with a lazy Susan. It's just right the way it is."

"On rainy days, Consuelo puts a big blanket over it and lets me pretend it's a tent."

"Jeff, you need to quiet down," Nathan said matter-of-factly. "It's time to use your mouth to eat, not to talk."

As she dished rice onto her plate, Val piped up. "Yeah, well, Amber wasn't very quiet today, either. I wanted to crawl under the pew when she started in!"

Van muffled a laugh. "Nathan took care of it. And get this, Nathan: Eulla Mae and Harold came up to me in the narthex and thought it was hilarious that Amber wanted to make it a trio with them. They weren't upset in the least."

"Eulla Mae is gifted with grace," Mom said.

Nathan snorted. "I'm certainly not."

His words stunned Vanessa for a moment until she followed his rueful gaze. He'd managed to drop a shrimp, and it had slithered away from the serving spoon, leaving a thin, messy, pinkish streak across the table.

"You can't escape me!" Vanessa nabbed it with her fork. "Ta da! Gotcha, you little rascal."

"Catching a shrimp isn't a big deal. I wish you woulda gotten a whale." Jeff's lower lip poked out in a classic pout. "I didn't get to see no whale on our trip."

"No, we didn't get to see any whales, but we did see lots of cool sea creatures yesterday at the tide pools," Nathan reminded him. "You saw anemones and urchins and hermit crabs. . . ."

"Van? Dad said we can go back to the tide pools again. Wanna come with us?"

"I'd love to!"

After the meal was over, Nathan swiped the check and paid the bill. They all walked out to the parking lot, and after he left, Dad and Mom bracketed Vanessa.

"Honey, he's a good man," Mom said.

"But he's not walking with the Lord," Dad said. "He's

fallen away. I hate to see you get more deeply involved. It's a big mistake."

"Involved? It's friendship. And for the record, I have a deal with Nathan. He knows he has a standing invitation to come to church, but I don't bug him. Today was the first time in five years he's attended church, and I'm thankful for that answer to prayer."

"We're glad he came. We hope he continues, but Van, don't start wading into 'missionary dating.' You know it's wrong."

"Yeah. I understand. Just notice that it was Jeff who asked me to go to the tide pools—not Nathan."

Inside, she felt a niggling about that fact. She really wished Nathan had asked. . . Then again, she was glad he hadn't—not because of her family's misgivings, but because she didn't want to have to start examining her feelings about him too closely. Deep down, she knew full well if he was an on-fire believer—*No. I'm not going there. This is about God and His relationship with Nathan. I'm not in the picture. I'm not. Well, okay, so I am—but just a little bit.*

fifteen

"You want me to what?" Vanessa stopped dead in her tracks on the aisle between the birdseed and kitty litter. Her hand wrapped around the cordless phone receiver more tightly. Amber stood patiently at her side, oblivious to the ridiculous suggestion Nathan had just made.

"Jeff mentioned it the other day at lunch—the tide pools. Why are you sounding so surprised?"

"I'm not exactly surprised you asked, but—"

"You're off on Monday, and I'm at a point in my projects that I can take a day off too. Jeff's school booked a student-free day for the teachers, so he won't miss any class."

"So far, I'm fine with that—"

"You also said Amber is allowed there," he tempted without taking a breath, "so that's not a hitch."

Vanessa marveled at his delivery. He'd reasoned out all of the contingencies and her possible objections and delivered his sales pitch as smoothly as he banged a nail into place with a hammer. She grimaced. He'd failed to take one major point into account.

"C'mon, Van. Whadda ya say?"

Vanessa stuffed an outdated tablet of rebate coupons in the trash can under the counter. "You were doing fine until you started discussing high and low tides."

"You have to get there right as the tide is going out so you can see the best assortment of all of the sea life. Those first hours are awesome!"

"I have to be awake so I can see." She wiped off the counter and headed toward the kittens' cage. She'd sold all but two of them, and they looked like they could both use some attention. "I couldn't pry my eyes open at 6:43 if you dropped a python on me."

Nathan chuckled.

"I don't really even think," she mused as she dangled a feather teaser toy at one of the fluff balls, "the world is alive yet at that hour."

"It is. I assure you, it is."

"I'll take your word for it." She laughed at his impatient snort as well as at the kittens' antics. "I'm not about to actually discover that for myself."

"You already have. When you bailed me out that night, Jeff had you up by six-thirty."

"Boy, oh, boy. I do a guy a favor, and he tosses it right back in my face."

"It's a good cause. Think about how disappointed Jeff was when we didn't spot any whales when we went whale watching. A trip to the tide pools will help make up for it."

"Nathan, you already took him."

"But you weren't there."

"Yeah, well, it's a safe bet that I'm going to be a no-show for anything that requires me to crawl out of bed before sunrise. My alarm clock and I have an ironclad agreement: It doesn't wake me up before 7:23, and I keep it plugged in."

"7:23?"

"And not a second sooner. I have a routine all worked out so I can stay in bed until the very last minute." She tossed a jingly bell in for the kittens and fastened the cage's catch. "I told you I'm a night owl."

"You're not exaggerating at all?"

"Okay, I confess—Val dragged me out of bed and poured coffee into me so I'd make seven-thirty classes in high school and college."

"So you can get up and function."

"Not really. She and I are polar opposites—she's a lark, and I'm an owl. It's probably one of the reasons she got As and I didn't in all of those crack-of-dawn classes. I was just sleep-walking with a commuter mug in my hand."

"Ah ha!" His baritone laughter rippled over the phone line. "I've discovered your weakness. Jeff and I will bring a giant mug of coffee for you."

"Not good enough."

"No? Jeff will be so disappointed, Van. He really wanted you and Amber to go with us."

"Life is made up of all sorts of little disappointments." If anything, Nathan sounded rather downhearted himself. She couldn't tamp down her smile, even though he couldn't see her. "Chocolate has caffeine, you know."

"You'd eat chocolate at six in the morning?"

"As far as I'm concerned, if I'm breathing, it's a good time to eat chocolate. I'm a firm believer in eating my vegetables, and cocoa is a bean."

Nathan spluttered for a moment, then recovered wryly, "I suppose that is an example of the kind of stuff you, ah, 'learned' in one of those early morning science classes."

"The benefits of a good education." She laughed. "I probably ought to set a good example for Jeff, though. I'll settle for hot cocoa."

"Great! We'll pick you up at six on Monday."

"Six-fifteen." After she hung up, Vanessa put the phone back on the base and folded her arms akimbo. "That man missed his calling in life. He should have gone into retail sales where he'd get a hefty commission. He'd be rolling in the dough in less than a month."

Amber looked up at her as if she understood and agreed with every last word.

"Come on, Girl. We have work to do." Amber stood and followed along as Vanessa went along the aisle with all of her fish tanks. She sprinkled food along the surface of the water and watched as the fish tumbled about in the water like colorful sprinkles in a kaleidoscope.

When she and Val had worked here when they were in college, she'd hated cleaning out the fish tanks. It was a slimy, messy, smelly job. Her boss really liked fish, though. Pete would stand and admire the nearly translucent fins, the way the colors went iridescent, and the grace with which the fish cruised through the tanks. He'd actually had a second aisle of exotics. She'd gotten accustomed to caring for them.

All along, she'd thought to go into veterinary medicine—well, until she'd gotten into anatomy and physiology. She'd sat in the corner of the lab and tried to force herself to participate, but she couldn't dissect the cat. It looked just like Elvira, the sleek black cat she and Val had for several years. As a compromise, she'd done her "dissection" on a computer instead. When she went to turn in all of the necessary pages, Dr. Bainbridge was visiting her professor.

Her professor made a disparaging comment, but Dr. Bainbridge came to her defense. He'd been the family vet for Elvira; the poodle, Fluff; and later her first guide puppy, Thane. He'd gently suggested she was excellent at caring for healthy animals—perhaps she ought to think about running a pet store or kennel instead of going into veterinary medicine. He'd even put in a good word with Pete at the pet store, who promptly hired both Van and Val.

Val had enjoyed running the register, pricing things, and keeping the books. Van, on the other hand, had gone wild over the animals. She'd groomed them, played with them, kept the pens and cages spotless, and found tremendous satisfaction in helping customers find the perfect pet.

Pete had often remarked his business took off once the twins worked there. He chalked it up to their beauty. Van teased it was because Val finally straightened out his books so he could keep track of his funds. Val declared it was due to Vanessa's knack for selling not only the pet, but all of the necessary start-up gear. Whatever the truth, the job had paid for the rest of their schooling, and Pete had happily set their work schedules around the hours they needed off for classes.

Pete had waited until Van was almost ready to graduate before he told her he was thinking of selling his pet shop. Just the year before, Grandma had passed on and left a sizable legacy to her and Val. Val used her share to buy the condo. Van prayed and felt the Lord was opening doors. . . .

But not fish tanks.

She'd bought the store, renamed it, and promptly sold off half of the stock of fish. Now, she had five shiny tanks full of freshwater fish. Adding more puppies, dog chow, and gear made the store far more profitable—and she didn't have to clean as many tanks.

Nonetheless, the goldfish tank qualified as essential equipment. She often donated coupons to schools and the church to give to children for a free goldfish. Frequently those children came back to get another fish, or their parents bought inexpensive little aquarium accessories. When that family felt ready to get a different pet, they frequently came back to Whiskers, Wings, and Wags because they were familiar with it. Vanessa smiled to herself. Nathan and Jeff were the record holders for the shortest turnaround time.

Van polished a few fingerprints off the front of the last glass-fronted tank and watched the fish dart around. No doubt Jeff would want to know why she didn't stock sea urchins, sea stars, and hermit crabs. Under her breath, she murmured, "Nathan, your kid is as cute as you are."

❧

Sunday morning, Nathan set out cereal and grabbed a banana for Jeff. It was the last one—good thing too. It had reached the eat-now-or-toss-it stage. They needed to do some grocery shopping. Nathan would rather haggle with a city inspector over a building variance than walk the aisles of the grocery store. Jeff always wanted to buy all the junk food he'd seen advertised. Invariably, Nathan would skip a row or two just to get out of the place faster, only to stand at the register and remember something he needed and hadn't seen.

There were times when he thought about asking Consuelo if she'd take on the grocery shopping and cook suppers, but that went against one of the lessons he wanted to teach Jeff. A man could get some help with a few things—even delegate—but overall it was important to be capable of coping with issues. Someday his son would have to face life on his own. Nathan knew he needed to equip Jeff with skills like shopping and, well, basic stuff like opening cans and nuking frozen junk in a microwave.

He took a swig from his mug and made a wry face. The aroma barely qualified as coffee, and the taste didn't. He'd used the last few spoons of grounds out of the bottom of the can to make this pot. He scribbled "coffee" on the shopping list and underlined it.

"Sport, turn off those cartoons and come eat. We've got stuff to do today."

"We do?" Jeff had been lying on the floor next to Lick, watching TV. He stood and pushed the off button.

"Yeah. I'm gonna hop in the shower. I already poured milk on your cereal, so it'll get mushy if you don't eat it right away."

Nathan walked up the stairs and climbed into the shower. As he scrubbed, he made a mental list of other things he should have put on the grocery list and forgotten. He'd yanked up his jeans when Jeff traipsed in, covered from neck to toes with mud. "What happened to you?"

"Lick wanted out. You told me to be sure to let him out right away any time he wanted to go so he wouldn't have any accidents."

"I fenced off the dirt in the backyard, though." As he spoke, Nathan stripped Jeff out of his clothes and shoved him into the shower.

Jeff's scrawny little chest puffed out with pride. "Lick wanted to go out the front door."

"You didn't—"

"He was really good, Dad. He did his business, and when he started to run away, I called 'Come!' to him, just like Van told me to. He turned around and came right away."

"Let me guess: The living room is as muddy as you are."

"Nope." His grin took on a decidedly cocky flair. "I helped Lick wipe off his paws on the doormat."

"Judging from your clothes, he thought you were the doormat. Clean all of that off."

As his son showered, Nathan finished dressing and tossed the muddy clothes into his hamper. Consuelo did laundry—a chore for which he happily paid her extra. She'd definitely earn her money with that load. Nathan knew she wouldn't bat an eye at it. The clothes he wore to construction sites often came back equally gritty.

Thank God for Consuelo.

He stopped dead in his tracks. He couldn't remember the last time he'd actually been thankful to the Lord. In this case, he had to confess, it was a heartfelt emotion. Without her, he wouldn't have made it through the last five years.

"Dad?"

"What, Sport?"

"It's Sunday, right?"

"Yep." He globbed a dab of toothpaste on his brush, started to work on his molars, and froze. He caught sight of Jeff in the bathroom mirror. His son had pulled back the shower curtain and looked at him with hope shining in his big brown eyes.

"Can I go to Sunday school?"

Slowly Nathan pulled the toothbrush from his mouth. He spat in the sink, then turned around. "You already went to Sunday school last week."

"Unh-huh. It was fun."

"Why do the same thing again?" He hoped he sounded casual. This wasn't in his plan. He'd thought it would be a one-shot deal, then Jeff would latch onto some other activity. Normally, he grew distracted or bored and moved on to a new thing.

"We're going to the tide pools again. You told me we'd see different creatures. The Sunday school teacher told me they hear a new story every week, so it'll be different there too."

Miscalculated on that score, Adams. Now what're you gonna do?

"Listen, Sport—I thought maybe we'd go out for—"

"Lunch with Vanessa and her family again? Yippee!" Jeff disappeared behind the shower curtain.

Nathan turned back to the sink and ordered, "Wash behind your ears." He looked at his reflection. A thin line of toothpaste outlined the center of his lower lip. Deep, harsh grooves bracketed his mouth. *What have I gotten myself into?*

sixteen

Nathan sat in the sanctuary and thumbed the edge of the bulletin. Jeff was so excited about going to Sunday school, he'd gotten ready in record time, and they'd arrived a bit early. Nathan sat in the same pew he'd occupied last week. He hoped Van wouldn't be in the choir today. She could sit next to him and make it so he didn't feel quite so lonely or out of place.

Last week, the organ music made the hair on the back of his neck prickle. Today, the softly played hymn flowed over his nerves. It fit his mood like his favorite hammer just kind of fit in his hand when he was working on a project around the house.

The bulletin featured the morning's hymns and Scripture, then had another segment, "Looking Forward." It listed all the upcoming activities and events. He smiled as he noticed the last ball game of the season was listed. A plea for tools and willing hands for building a church in Mexico piqued his interest a little. *What am I thinking? I didn't even want to go to church. Why would I get involved in a project like that?* He swiftly turned the bulletin over.

LOOKING AROUND mentioned a birth, a wedding, and the names of those who were or had been in the hospital. Fair enough. It was nice to see this place really functioned like a cohesive church family—really caring for its own.

There was one last little section LOOKING BACK. It simply asked, "How was your walk this week?"

Nathan drew in a sharp breath. He set aside the bulletin and wished he hadn't read those words. *How was my walk? My walk? God, I'm the walking wounded.* He bowed his head in weariness. *This week.* The last two words of the question echoed in his mind. This week? This week had gone better than. . .well, than since he'd torn out of church five years ago. The realization stopped him cold. It really had been a better week. Less empty. Not the same struggle. But why? What had made the difference?

"Nice to see you here, Adams."

Nathan looked to the side and stood at once. He shook hands with Bill Zobel and glanced down at Amber. "What happened? You're missing all but one of your gals."

"Ellen volunteers in the nursery once a month. Val is working this weekend. Someone at work is sick, so she's been putting in a lot of extra days and overtime."

"That's a bummer." He tried to sound casual and fought the urge to look around. "What about Vanessa?"

"She'll be here in a minute. She made cupcakes for a bake sale, and I'd rather baby-sit Amber than carry a tray of food. I'd either accidentally dump it on someone or eat half of them before I reached the kitchen."

"You have more self-control than I do, because I've tasted her cupcakes. I'd have eaten all of them." The small talk wasn't exactly difficult, but Nathan knew he didn't measure up to Bill's dreams for his daughter's future husband. Granted, Bill behaved more than just cordially. Vanessa must have inherited her friendly, outgoing nature from him. Even so, there was a world of difference between accepting someone as a friend and welcoming him as the man who was dating your daughter.

Nathan wanted to sit at the edge of the pew so he could simply scoot over to allow Van to take that place and be close to Amber. With Bill standing there, he'd have to scoot in farther and have Bill sit between them. *It's probably exactly what he wants.*

"Your boy liked Chinese last Sunday. How do the two of you do with Italian?"

"I love it; Jeff wears it." Nathan grinned. "You saw him with the chow mein noodles last week. He's worse with spaghetti."

Bill chuckled. "How 'bout we all go out to Ruffino's for lunch?"

"Sounds good."

"I pick up the tab this time."

"Hi, guys!" Vanessa slipped up and gave her dad a hug.

It was a sweet sight. Vanessa was an affectionate woman, and her warmth never seemed out of place or forced. The way she acted around her family made Nathan think of how long it had been since he'd been on the receiving end of any such fondness. Sure, Jeff and he hugged and wrestled around—but the sentimentality a woman put into a hug—that was different. How would it feel to wrap his arms around Vanessa and have her put her arms back around him? To hold and be held—even for a fleeting moment? Five long years of not wanting any such contact ended abruptly, and the realization shook him. *Being in church really has me off balance.*

"Did I hear you say something about Ruffino's? I can already taste the veal scaloppini."

"Songs and sermon before the scaloppini." Bill pushed her closer to Nathan and glanced at his watch. "I forgot to sign up for the men's pancake prayer breakfast. I'm going to duck back and do that before the service starts. I'd be happy to have you as my guest, Nathan. It's Wednesday. What do you say?"

Nathan thought for a moment, then pulled a small palm computer from his pocket to check on a date. "I have a site inspection Wednesday morning." He felt an unexpected twinge of regret and paused for a second before proposing, "Maybe another time?"

"I'll hold you to that."

❧

Vanessa hummed all afternoon at the pet shop. *He came to church today! Two weeks in a row, he's come and heard the Word. Lord, please do a mighty work in Nathan's heart. There used to be a bitterness about him, but now there's just a sadness. Leech away the grief and pour Your love out on him.*

The bell at the door chimed. Patsy Dinnit zipped into the shop with her pedigreed Border collie on a hot pink, rhinestone-studded leash. "Van! Jazzy's going to have a litter. Do you want to take the puppies on commission again?"

"Amber, stay." Vanessa left her and went around to the other side of the counter. Amber normally did well around other dogs, but Jazzy tended to act high-strung when she carried a litter.

Stooping to give Jazzy a couple of strokes, Van asked, "Did you use the same sire? The last litter was gorgeous."

"Sure did! Sire's owner would get pick of the litter, but you can have all of the rest. I'll do an even split on the proceeds with you again."

"Let me grab my calendar and see what I have booked. When is she due?"

"In about four weeks."

Vanessa went back to the register. "Good girl." She patted Amber and reached for her calendar. "That would make it about the twenty-eighth, give or take a few days." She then flipped two pages. "If I take them when they're about eight weeks, that'll be in August. I have dachshunds and Labs coming in about the same time. That'll be a nice variety."

A secretive smile lit Patsy's face. She looked this way

and that, then whispered, "Jazzy's not the only one who's expecting."

"Patsy! Really? How wonderful!"

"You have no idea what a miracle it is. Hugo and I have been trying to have a baby for almost four years. I'm so excited, I can hardly stand it. I haven't said a word to anyone until today. We went and had an ultrasound Friday. Wanna see the picture?"

"I'd love to! When are you due?"

"January second. Hugo is already talking to the baby. Last night, he tapped my belly and told the kid to come early so we'd have a tax deduction!"

"Oh, no!" Vanessa giggled. "It's a good thing Hugo and Val didn't fall in love and get married. They're both so into business and accounting, they'd breed a whole tribe of bean counters."

Patsy gave an exaggerated wince. "They'd name them Lima and Chili."

"Those beans have some class. I was thinking more along the line of Jelly—can't you see it now?" Vanessa spread her hands in the air like she was holding up a banner. "Jelly Dinnit."

Patsy gave her a mock look of hurt and rubbed her still-flat tummy. "How could you say such a thing? I planned for something more affectionate. . .Sugar. Sugar Dinnit."

"I just finished lunch, but this is making me hungry!"

"I saw you go into Ruffino's with that gorgeous hunk. Who is he? He was at church last week too. You work fast, Girl!"

"He's just a friend. We met my family there. I sold him a dog, and he's taking obedience training."

"He is, or the dog?" Patsy gave her an impish wink.

Vanessa waggled her forefinger at Patsy. "Your husband is going to have his hands full if this baby is half as spunky as you are."

"You're calling me spunky? Ha! Now you—your kids are

going to be balls of fire."

"Predictions like that are enough to make me stay a spinster."

"Not a chance. That guy—you and he are going to be an item. I can feel it in my bones. Mark my words: In a few months, you're going to be gliding down the aisle."

"Me? Glide? Only if I were on a skateboard. You're mixing me up with Val. She'll glide, for sure. If you see me going down the aisle, it'll be in a bridesmaid's gown."

"Nope. You're not going to dissuade me. It's my vision, and the groom was that fine-looking man you sat next to in church."

"You know. . ." Vanessa tapped her cheek and looked at the ceiling, as if lost in important thoughts. "I seem to recall prophets who are wrong are put to death. You're so wrong about any entanglement there, it's downright dangerous."

Patsy giggled and dug through her purse for the picture of the ultrasound. "Look at this. This is a miracle."

Vanessa turned it around and looked at the wedge-shaped picture. "Amazing. Just amazing. Look! I can make out his profile! Is it a him or a her?"

"We told them not to tell us. It's so delicious, just knowing we're having a baby. I like leaving that secret in God's hands until He puts this baby in ours."

"Oh, yes. Like Psalm 139 talks about Him creating us in our mother's womb. I'm so thrilled for you. What a blessing."

Patsy agreed and carefully tucked away the ultrasound picture. She smiled. "That is my blessing and good news. I'm standing by what I said earlier, though. Go ahead and call it dangerous thinking, but I'm sure you and that guy are going to be an item."

Patsy left, and Vanessa looked down at Amber. "Dangerous. Even thinking Nathan could ever change and find me attractive is so far from possible, I'd be a fool to waste my time considering it." She turned and saw her reflection in the shop-window. *Am I looking at a fool?*

❧

The alarm clock went off, and Nathan groaned. He'd been lying awake for the last twenty minutes, hoping the rain would stop. Instead, it kept falling. If anything at all, it seemed to be intensifying. There was no way they could go to the tide pools in this kind of weather. Reluctantly, he picked up the phone and dialed.

" 'Lo?"

"Hey, Sleepyhead, it's raining."

"You woke me up to give a weather report?"

"We won't be able to go to the tide pools." He sat up and stacked several coins on his bedside table. Jeff would come in and swipe them. He loved to plink the dimes, nickels, and pennies into the enormous, multicolored plastic dinosaur-egg bank in the corner of his bedroom.

"Nathan Adams," Vanessa moaned over the phone, "you are rotten to the core. Cruel. Mean. There probably isn't a person on the face of the earth more vile than you." Her bed squeaked, and her blankets made a loud ruffling noise, tattling that she'd rolled over.

He smiled at how zany, impulsive Van could be so pre-dictable about this one particular aspect of life. She'd been more than honest when she confessed she wasn't a morning person. "Need another minute to wake up?"

"Wake up? Why?" She yawned. "I'm going right back to sleep as soon as I tell you how barbaric you are to dare calling me at this ridiculous hour."

"Come on, Van. You can't be mad."

She yawned again—a long, luxurious, stretched sound that let him know she could easily shut her eyes and coast right back off.

"You were going to wake up now, anyway," he wheedled shamelessly.

"Not really. I had it all planned out. I'd get dressed, sleep in your car, and sleepwalk on the beach. Amber would rescue me if I accidentally walked into the surf."

"Don't forget that plan. We'll put it into play some other day." Nathan swept the quarters into the jar beside his bed for the once-a-month pilgrimage he and Jeff took to an arcade. The arcade! His heart galloped in anticipation. He'd come up with a great substitute for them. "I have an alternative plan for the day."

"It better start with, 'Van, sleep in 'til noon.'"

"Eight."

"Eleven." Her voice still sounded husky with sleep.

"Nine, and you still get hot chocolate."

Vanessa muttered something unintelligible and hung up the phone.

"Dad?" Jeff stood in the doorway, curling his toes on the cold, hardwood floor. "You promised we'd go to the tide pools again to see the sea creatures today."

Nathan opened his arms, and Jeff scampered across the room and launched into a hug. Nathan held his son, rubbed his bristly cheek in Jeff's sleep-mussed hair, and growled like a bear.

Jeff giggled and wrapped his arms as far around Nathan's chest as they'd reach. He paused a second, then asked in a sad tone, "Papa Bear, what're we gonna do? Vanessa and Amber wanted to go to the beach with us."

"I know you're disappointed, but I have a plan. . . ."

seventeen

"It's rain-ing, it's pour-ing, the old man is snor-ing."

Vanessa stared at Nathan and Jeff as they stood on her doorstep. She yanked them through her door. "Are the two of you crazy? Standing in the rain, singing. . ."

She paused, then huffed, "Without me? Seriously. I'm hurt."

Nathan closed his huge black-and-gray-striped golf umbrella with a loud snap. Jeff continued to sing as water dripped off his bright yellow slicker. He fiddled with one of the fasteners. " 'Nessa, d'you know that song?"

"Yep. Val and I used to sing it when we were little. I forgot all about it." She looked at Nathan and frowned. A water-splattered plastic grocery bag hung from the crook of his elbow. "What is that?"

"Your hot chocolate, Madame." He opened the bag and pulled out a carton of chocolate milk with a flourish.

"Nathan, I hate to break it to you, but that isn't hot."

He gave her a supercilious look. "Not yet, it isn't. My faithful sidekick, Master Jeffrey, will assist me in the delicate operation of preparing it for you." He helped Jeff peel out of his slicker and cleared his throat. "Come along, young man. We have serious work to do."

"Oh, boy. This I've gotta see." Vanessa tagged along behind them as they headed into her kitchen.

"Pop fly!" Nathan picked up his son and sat him on the kitchen counter.

"Pop fly?" Vanessa echoed. "How'd you come up with that saying?"

"It's from baseball, Silly," Jeff said.

"And I'm his pop, and I made him fly." Nathan opened a cupboard, shook his head, and shut it.

Vanessa didn't say a word. She backed against the counter on the far side of the kitchen so she'd be out of the way and still have a bird's-eye view of the goings-on. Nathan opened the next cupboard and shot her a quick look over his shoulder. "Wow, this is impressive. Even if we hadn't tasted some of your goodies already, all of this junk in here tells me you make more than just cupcakes on a pretty regular basis."

She shrugged. "I like to bake."

"I like to eat!" Jeff gave her a greedy smile.

Nathan's smile matched it perfectly. "Me, too! Especially your stuff. We're willing to sacrifice our taste buds and stomachs to the cause anytime."

"I'll keep that in mind."

The third cupboard held the coffee mugs Nathan wanted. He pulled out the first one with a wave worthy of a game-show host. "Ta da!"

"You didn't have to search. I could have just told you where they were."

"Oh, but this is an adventure, and Master Jeffrey and I are sleuths."

"I hate to break the news, but sleuths are for mysteries, not adventures."

Vanessa watched Nathan get out more mugs and unbutton the sleeves of his tan-and-green plaid flannel shirt. He methodically rolled up those sleeves, revealing muscular forearms. He then did the same thing to the sleeves on Jeff's little blue denim shirt. He made quite a production of it, as if they were about to make a seven-course gourmet meal instead of heat up chocolate milk. Vanessa couldn't decide whether the show was for her or for Jeff. Either way, she enjoyed every last second.

Nathan scrounged up a saucepan, set it on the range, then ordered, "Son, find a spoon. I'll need to stir this."

Jeff turned onto his belly on the counter, reached over the edge, and jerked open the drawer. The silverware in it jangled. "Dad, do you want a big spoon or a little spoon?"

"A little one," Nathan said as he wrestled with the milk carton. It didn't open neatly. Instead, the waxed cardboard wouldn't separate, so he scowled at the carton as if his dark look would make it cooperate.

Vanessa watched the whole process with nothing short of delight. *I would have gotten up at six for this show. This is a riot.*

Nathan gave up on the first side of the milk carton and attacked the other side. It yielded.

Probably out of fear.

He poured the chocolate milk into the saucepan and dumped the mangled carton into the trash with more emphasis than the poor thing deserved. When Nathan turned back around, he gave Jeff a blank stare. "What is that?"

"A little spoon."

Vanessa bit the inside of her lip to keep from laughing as Jeff held out the quarter teaspoon from a set of measuring spoons that had gotten separated.

"When we look in my toolbox, you know how I have the great big mallet, and I have the regular hammers, then I have that skinny, little finishing hammer?"

"Dad, you're not going to stir the hot chocolate with a hammer, are you?"

Vanessa started laughing.

Nathan shot her a disgruntled look, then suddenly perked up. "Yes, Sport, I am. See?" He took two strides, came close enough to Vanessa for her to inhale his expensive, spicy aftershave, and reached around her. He snagged her meat-tenderizing mallet and nodded. Holding it high, he declared,

"Always be sure to use the right tool for the job, Jeff."

Humor mingled with disbelief as Vanessa watched Nathan hold on to the business end of the mallet, dunk the handle into the saucepan, and proceed to stir. She had to give him credit. He'd managed to recover pretty smoothly.

"Dad, what am I s'posed to do with this little spoon?"

"Yeah, Nathan," she chimed in. "What's that bitsy spoon for?"

"That is. . ." He paused for a split second. "The tasting spoon. Yes, the tasting spoon. Whoever holds the tasting spoon has the important job of deciding when the hot chocolate is ready."

Vanessa dug out three mismatched party napkins from the pantry and put them on the table. Soon Nathan set the cups of steaming cocoa on the table. He dumped a telephone book onto a chair to act as a booster seat for Jeff, and they were ready. The rich scent of hot chocolate filled the air, and Vanessa curled her fingers around the mug. She stopped short when Jeff drummed his fingers on the table.

"Aren't we gonna say a prayer?"

❧

Nathan froze. He hadn't seen that coming, but he should have. Vanessa always took a moment to pray. For the past two Sundays, her father had prayed over the lunches. A man should be the spiritual head of the home. . .the adage went through his mind. *It's not my home,* he tried to reason, but that excuse sounded pathetic. There had once been a time when speaking to the Lord came so naturally, so freely. Now here he sat, mute.

"When I was a little girl," Vanessa said to Jeff, "I learned some prayers. Maybe you'd like to learn one of them. You can say the words after me."

"That's a good idea." Nathan breathed a silent sigh of relief. Listening to Jeff's pure voice repeat each phrase after Vanessa did something odd to Nathan. *Evie would have wanted this. She wanted our son to grow up in the Lord. She wanted me to fall in love again and live a full life. How many times did she tell me that? I didn't believe her. I refused to listen because I couldn't bear to think of going on without her—but I have. I've had to, mostly for Jeff. But now I want to for me. Thank you, Evie, for being so sweet to give me your blessing to move on. Had you known Vanessa, you would have been good friends.*

In those moments, Nathan sensed a momentous shift. He had a past, but he wanted a future. For five long years, he'd not looked ahead. Now he saw a bridge in the guise of a simple child's prayer.

Am I using God and religion as a way of making it acceptable to court and love Vanessa? I've done nothing but shake my fist in God's face for five years. Now, suddenly, I'm going to do this turnabout? How convenient is that? Is this a matter of my heart or of my soul?

"Da—ad. You're not listening."

"What?" Nathan snapped out of his contemplation.

"I asked you when you were going to tell Van about where we're going."

"If Van is willing to watch you, I'm going to Mexico."

"What about the arcade, Dad? I wanna play games!"

Nathan looked at Vanessa. "We'll play at the arcade today, but if that hammer in Vanessa's kitchen is anything like the ones going to Mexico, that team needs a lot of help to build that church."

"Why can't I go with you?"

"It's a school week." Nathan took a gulp of hot cocoa. He needed to get away to think. Vanessa needed time to be with Jeff to see if they could get along well for more than just a day at a time.

A short while later, while Jeff smacked buttons on a blaring machine at the arcade and Amber sat patiently at Vanessa's side, Nathan apologized. "I should have asked you privately about watching Jeff instead of blurting it out like that. If you'd rather not, I'll understand."

She hitched a shoulder and laughed self-consciously. "Oh—I'm happy to watch him. He's a lot of fun. I was trying to find a way of suggesting it might be easier if I stayed at your place with him than bringing Lick to mine."

"You wouldn't mind?"

"Why should I?"

"It's closer to the school, but it'll be farther for you to get to and from work."

She hitched the strap of her purse up onto her shoulder. "I'm glad you're going to go. The team needs guys like you who know what you're doing. You have a lot of talent. It's generous of you to want to use it for G—" She caught herself. "For others."

Nathan slid his hand over hers and laced their fingers. Her eyes widened. "I need a chance to do some soul-searching and thinking."

"I got hundreds of points and this many tickets on that game!" Jeff half shouted the words and intruded on the moment. He stood before them and held up a long trail of pale blue rafflelike tickets the arcade machine spit out. "I wanna get so many, I can get something really cool."

"Oh, is that so?" Vanessa broke away and rose. "I'm lethal on Uranium Thief."

"Can I play you? Can I?"

"You'd better. I'd be horribly disappointed to come all of the way here with you and not get a chance to razzle dazzle you with my ability."

"Oh, brother," Nathan scoffed. "Jeff, can you believe her?

She really thinks she knows what she's doing, but she doesn't know who she's playing against."

Vanessa's chin went up at a stubborn tilt. "I challenge you here and now—and if I get to the third level before you, you have to eat a fried pickle."

"A fried pickle?" Nathan and Jeff said together.

Vanessa dusted her hands together. "A fried pickle. Now prepare for doom. You're about to wish you'd never brought me along today."

"Even if I have to eat a fried pickle, I won't feel doomed." Nathan looked at her intently. "I'd never be glad that you hadn't come along."

eighteen

"Twenty-eight dollars?" Vanessa twisted in the seat and gave Nathan an appalled look. "We wasted twenty-eight dollars at the arcade?"

"It wasn't a waste, Vanessa. We had a good time, didn't we?"

"And look at all of the good stuff I earned!" Jeff sat in the middle of the backseat like Midas in the center of his golden treasures. He'd spent half of forever choosing bouncy balls, slink chains, squirt guns, a magnifying glass, crazy sunglasses, candy, and half a dozen other assorted "prizes" with the tickets he'd earned from the arcade machines. Had they gone to a five-and-dime, he could have bought all of it for five bucks, max. Nevertheless, they'd had fun, and his pride made it all worthwhile.

"Sport, here's that big, big bridge."

"Are we going on it? Really?"

"No kidding."

Jeff sat a little straighter and craned to look out over the very edge of the bridge.

The railing came up so high that Vanessa could barely see over it part of the time. The Coronado Bridge in San Diego swept in a huge, graceful, sideways arc. It boasted such height, military vessels passed under it with ease. This kind of height gave her a sense of freedom. She tried to concentrate on looking as far out at whatever horizon she could spot through the drizzle. Due to the weather, there wasn't the usual abundance of sailboats out.

Charming, little old houses covered the island. Well-manicured lawns and nicely sculpted shrubs reflected the orderly community of military officers and understated wealthy citizens. Vanessa watched a cat streak across a lawn and shoot up a tree.

"Oh! I was so busy gawking, I didn't notice we passed the restaurant. I'm sorry, Nathan. It was on the left back there."

He gave her a startled look. "You're serious."

"Of course I am. I blew it."

"No problem—that can happen to anyone. I meant, you're serious about that restaurant—that it has fried pickles!"

She bobbed her head. "And you two are going to eat them. I got to level three first."

Nathan pulled into a parking lot. Vanessa wrinkled her nose. "What are we doing here?"

"Getting antacids. If I have to eat a fried pickle, I want something to rescue my stomach afterward."

"Hey! Don't knock it until you've tried it!"

"Ever hear of 'an ounce of prevention'? Well, I'm subscribing to that theory." Nathan opened his door. "I'll be back in a sec."

Ten minutes later, he emerged from the drugstore. He carried a big paper sack and stuck it between the two front seats. Vanessa peeped inside and let out a disbelieving laugh.

At least a full-dozen bottles of pink liquid jumbled in the bag.

"If you don't want to eat the fried pickles, just say so. You didn't have to buy out the store."

He snapped his seat belt and hitched his shoulder. "I figured we'd need it for the Mexico trip. Two for one."

"You're a bargain shopper? Who woulda thunk it?"

"Bargain? Me? You've got to be kidding. I'm not talking about a sale. I'm saying I'm killing two birds with one stone—the pickles and the trip."

Ten minutes later, seated in the Red Oak Steakhouse, Jeff repeated the prayer after Vanessa said each line. Just before she said, "amen", he blurted out, "And God, please don't let Daddy kill those birds. Amen."

"What birds, Son?"

Jeff gave his father a sad look. "The ones on your trip that you wanna throw rocks at."

"It's just a saying, Sport. It means taking care of two things at the same time."

"Oh."

Vanessa gave Jeff's hand a reassuring squeeze. "But you were right. You can pray about anything that bothers you. I do, and it makes me feel better."

Vanessa saw emotion flare in Nathan's eyes, but she couldn't interpret it.

"Your mom did that too," he said quietly to Jeff. "She talked to God about all sorts of things."

The food came, and Jeff practically dove across the table. "I wanna try the pickle!"

Vanessa arranged the napkin in her lap and avoided looking at Nathan. Had she gone too far? Spoken when she should have held her tongue? Opened the door to his grief again? Being torn between living for Christ and being sensitive to Nathan's limits was like being stuck between third base and home—she was in a pickle, all right.

❧

Nathan didn't want the day to end. More to the point, he didn't want his time with Vanessa to be over. After lunch, he decided they ought to take in a movie. They'd just missed the beginning, so to burn up time until the next showing, he drove to the huge, red-roofed Hotel Del Coronado. "Why don't we wander and gawk? This old place is fascinating."

"I need to stop at the desk and make sure they're okay with Amber on the premises."

"I'll drive up to the front, then." He pulled up to the entrance of the white main building, and a bellhop immediately opened Vanessa's door.

"I'll only be a minute." She hopped out, and Amber started to follow. "Amber, stay."

When Vanessa slipped inside, Nathan reached down and petted the dog. "She'll be right back."

Indeed Vanessa came right back out. A gust of wind blew her hair into wild disarray, but Nathan could see her laugh in delight rather than become upset. She found so much joy in simple things. He loved that about her. She ducked her head into the car. "They're fine with Amber as long as I have the training jacket and gentle leader on her. How about if Jeff and Amber stay with me while you park? That way we won't have wet fur and a soggy boy?"

Nathan looked beyond the portico at the gloomy drizzle and shook his head. As he scooted out of the car, he said, "I'll just have them valet park. That way, we'll all stay dry, and we'll be able to get back to the theater on time."

They entered the lobby, and Vanessa started to get the giggles. Nathan gave her a questioning look. "What's come over you?"

"The valet is going to see all of those bottles you bought at the drugstore and think I'm the world's worst cook!"

"You're a good cook, Van," Jeff piped up. "I like the stuff you make, and you know how to make lotsa different junk. Dad's a pretty good cook too. He makes terrific hot chocolate!"

"Sport, you need to use your indoor voice." Nathan looked around. "So where do you want to go first?"

Vanessa looked around. "We can go downstairs and wander

through a few shops. If it's not raining, we can peek at the swimming pool."

Nathan nodded toward one of the antique elevators. The metal grillwork on it carried the grace of a bygone era. "They sure don't make beauties like that anymore. Should we give Amber a chance to ride?"

"Amber?" Jeff looked crestfallen. "What about me?"

Vanessa leaned down. "You get to be the tail guard. You come along and make sure her tail doesn't get caught in the door. That's an important job."

They spent a leisurely hour-and-a-half wandering around. Jeff kept twisting around to check on Amber's tail. "He's a responsible little guy," Vanessa praised.

When they got into the theater, Nathan used a small penlight he'd brought in from his glove compartment to illuminate the floor. They found a spot that didn't have any spilled soda or popcorn, and Amber curled up. Vanessa took her seat, and to Nathan's dismay, Jeff hopped into the seat right next to her. He thought about picking the boy up and plopping him down in the next seat over. That way, Nathan could slip his hand over and hold Vanessa's hand during the movie. . .or he could put his arm around her shoulders.

"No, that's not a good idea."

Nathan turned his head sharply. One of the men from the ball team held a flimsy cardboard tray laden with popcorn and drinks. He was trying to get four kids settled in and keep them from grabbing a drink all at the same time.

Nathan extended his arm and shored up the bottom of the tray. "You're about to lose the battle."

Doug groaned. "Thanks. Janey's mom and sister are in town. I volunteered to take all of the kids for the day—but that was when we had a clear weather report." He spied

Vanessa and gave Nathan a keen look.

Nathan ignored it. "Hope you enjoy the movie." He sat down. Had he needed to give a review of the movie, he'd be sunk. The whole time it played, Nathan tried to sort out his thoughts. He liked her. . .as more than just a friend. Somewhere along the way, she'd burrowed into his heart and made him start to face life again. He wanted her to be an integral part of that life. As the movie flickered on the screen, Nathan didn't even follow the plot. He came to the rock-solid conclusion that he wanted to make their relationship a public thing. . . and hopefully a very private thing too.

But wanting wasn't enough. Vanessa deserved someone who shared the joy and innocence of her beliefs, and Nathan didn't know if he could ever again be the man of faith he'd once been. Amber had howled during that hymn "It Is Well with My Soul," but Nathan had to admit, *It still isn't well with my soul.*

&

Two weeks later, Kip came into the pet shop. "Valene said you're going to watch Jeff so Nathan can go with the Mexico work-and-witness team. Knowing how clear he's been about not wanting to be involved with the church, I thought she got things mixed up. I couldn't imagine him hanging out with a bunch of us, building a sanctuary, of all things, but I just stopped by Seaside and got the paperwork. I'm sharing a tent with Nathan."

Vanessa stayed on her knees on the hard linoleum floor. She'd started cleaning the birdcages, and when she put the latest sheet of newspaper in the tray to line this one, she'd spotted the comic strips and had taken a moment to enjoy them.

Kip squatted down next to her. "Van, this isn't funny. I'm worried about you."

"You don't think I can handle Jeff and Lick for a week?"

"Stop it right there. You can play games and tease other people into changing a subject, but I know you too well to get sidetracked. You're losing your heart to Nathan." He held up a hand to keep Van from responding. "Don't bother to deny it or make excuses. It's a fact. The question is: What are you going to do about it?"

"Pray."

"That's a good first step. What about exercising some wisdom?"

Vanessa stared at Kip. He was known for being brutally honest at times. She had the sinking sensation she was about to get an earful. "I'm not going to pretend I'm at peace with everything, Kip. I'm being honest with God."

"But are you able to be honest with Him when you're not being honest with yourself?" He smacked his thigh in impatience. "I'm partially to blame. I told you to pursue the relationship because I hoped you might be the Lord's emissary to bring Nathan back into relationship with Him."

"You're not to blame, Kip. It's not that kind of situation at all. Since we're shooting straight from the hip, here's the truth: I really care for Nathan—as a friend and as a man. Until he can get over his grief and reestablish his relationship with the Lord, I know I can't let the relationship go any further."

"This whole thing bothers me a lot. Don't tell me you don't feel any hesitance, because you have to. Deep in your heart, you have to know God would want you to put a brake on this before it rolls out into dangerous territory."

Vanessa slid the tray back into the birdcage. "I was reading Philippians 4 today." She sat on the floor and quoted, " 'Let your gentle spirit be known to all men. The Lord is near. Be anxious for nothing, but in everything by prayer and supplication with thanksgiving let your requests be made known to God. And the peace of God, which surpasses all comprehension, will guard your hearts and your minds in Christ Jesus.' " She let out a prolonged sigh. "I have to trust the Lord with this. I need to be patient about His timing and believe that He'll guard my heart."

"Don't stop there. What about verses eight and nine?" He locked eyes with her and quoted, " 'Finally, brethren, whatever is true, whatever is honorable, whatever is right, whatever is pure, whatever is lovely, whatever is of good repute, if there is any excellence and if anything worthy of praise, dwell on these things. The things you have learned and received and heard and seen in me, practice these things, and the God of peace will be with you.' "

She waited. Tension sang between them.

"It's not right, and you know it isn't," Kip finally insisted. "Nathan hasn't renounced the Lord, but he's miles away from a strong walk. You're not feeling peace, and I think you need to reflect on it, because the Holy Spirit may be telling you to back off."

They both stood. Kip shook his head sadly. He reached over and cupped her cheek. "There was a time when I thought maybe you and I might make a go of things. I've always loved your sparkle and wit. I've accepted I won't ever be the man for you. You and Nathan have a special chemistry folks talk about that I've never really seen in action. I often struggle to tell you and Val apart when you're together; blindfolded, even as short a time as he's known you, he could figure out which one you are. I hoped maybe it was just infatuation and your family would step in and make you see the truth. I've probably put my foot in my mouth here, and you'll likely chalk all of this up to a wild, jealous rant. It's not, though. Van, as a brother in

Christ—and I know that's all I'll ever be—I felt compelled to speak the truth."

He patted her cheek, then pressed a chaste kiss on her forehead and walked out of the shop. The bell chimed over the door, and for once, its cheery noise seemed dreadfully out of place.

nineteen

Nathan stomped a few times and methodically dusted off his shirt front, sleeves, and the seat of his jeans before ducking into the tent. He was sore, dirty, and tired. He hadn't felt half as good in years.

"Place is really coming together," Kip said as he lounged on his sleeping bag. "We ought to be able to get the roof up tomorrow."

Nathan nodded. He rummaged through one of the athletic bags he'd brought, then pulled out a pair of granola bars. He tossed one at Kip. "I'm too hungry to wait for supper."

"I could eat the hind legs off a running buck." Kip chuckled as he peeled back the wrapper. "Who am I kidding? I'm getting so stiff, I couldn't catch a centipede."

"No more than anyone else."

Kip shook his head. "I was hoping playing ball would help get me back in shape. After all of that waiting at the hospital or sitting in a desk chair, I was pathetic."

"What were you at the hospital for?"

Kip set aside the Bible he'd been reading. "That was dumb of me. 'Course you wouldn't know. My sister had leukemia. She had a bone marrow transplant last year." He grinned. "She's doing great now."

"Wow. Bet your family feels pretty lucky."

"Blessed is a better word for it." He stretched and winced.

Nathan didn't say anything. For the past four nights, he'd stayed in the area after dinner for Bible study or fellowship. Around the fire they built in a big pit, they shared and spoke

f life's disappointments and joys, of how God gave them
rength in the hard times.

He'd learned Harriet, who was cooking all of their meals,
ormally took care of her mother with advanced Alzheimer's.
'ete and Lily had a daughter who was away at cystic fibrosis
amp. Hugo left Patsy at home, rejoicing in her pregnancy
fter they'd struggled in silence through several years of
nfertility. Ben's teenaged son was addicted to drugs.

Heartaches. Everyone has them. A little voice whispered,
But they turn to Me."

Kip grabbed a cell phone and toggled it in the air. "I'm due
o check in with the folks back home."

"I just called home, myself. Everything is fine."

"That's always good news. See you at chow." Kip left the tent.

Nathan looked at the Bible Kip left behind. He'd brought
is own. He hadn't read it in years. At first, it sat on the coffee
able, but he'd moved it to the dresser, then finally tucked it in
drawer. Out of sight, out of mind. While packing for this
rip, he'd tucked it in with his gear. He hadn't had the courage
o open it. Steeling himself, he pulled it out of his bag.

The unusually thick latigo cover still felt supple in his
ands. Sturdy. Enduring. *Unlike my faith.* He opened it up
nd braced himself for the pain. It didn't come. Instead, he
raced the lettering inside with a wash of gentle feelings.

With all the love God has given me for you, Evie.

She'd given it to him the Christmas they were engaged.
he'd fretted because the lettering went uphill slightly. He'd
ound it endearing. He'd told her it represented how they'd
lways look up.

*But I didn't. To the end, Evie clung to her faith. Me? I railed
t God, then hid away from Him.*

He thumbed through the gilt-edged pages. . .many marked
ith sermon notes or comments. The faded purple ribbon

placemarker lay with an odd twisted quirk at the center of Psalm 139.

Where can I go from Your Spirit? Or where can I flee from Your presence? If I ascend to heaven, You are there. If I make my bed in Sheol, behold, You are there. If I take the wings of the dawn, if I dwell in the remotest part of the sea, even there Your hand will lead me, and Your right hand will lay hold of me. If I say, "Surely the darkness will overwhelm me, and the light around me will be night," even the darkness is not dark to You, and the night is as bright as the day. Darkness and light are alike to You.

Nathan felt like he'd been punched in the gut. *I've been trying to hide, but it's impossible. In the darkness of my grief and anger, I was overwhelmed—but that was because I didn't look to the Light and hold fast to Him. People told me that, but I didn't listen.*

The memory of Lick's disobedience came back to him in a whole new light. He'd called, and Lick had ignored him; he'd commanded, and finally, when Lick did come, he'd petted and praised him—hoping it would make it easier for Lick to come back the next time. *And I've ignored God's voice. He's beckoned me, wooed me, called to me. . .yet He will still have a place for me like the father did for his prodigal son.*

"Nathan?" He hadn't heard Kip come back in the tent. Kip hunkered down beside him. "Do you need time alone, or do you need a brother right now?"

"I've been so bitter at God instead of holding fast to Him." His voice cracked. "I've been such a fool."

Kip sat down and gently pulled the Bible from him. He glanced down at the page, then looked up somberly. "David was a champion repenter. He messed up so many times. He went against God's will, but he knew the Lord's forgiveness was his if he confessed his sins and truly sought to restore his relationship. Is that how you're feeling?"

Tears burned Nathan's eyes. He barely choked out, "Yes."

Kip ran his stubby finger along the last verses of that chapter as he read aloud, "Search me, O God, and know my heart; Try me and know my anxious thoughts; And see if there be any hurtful way in me, And lead me in the everlasting way."

"That makes it all sound so simple."

"It is. You're complicating it. God knows you. He was waiting for you to turn to Him. His arms are wide open."

Someone slapped the side of the tent. "Supper's on!"

"Be there in a minute," Kip called.

Nathan grasped his hand. "Pray with me first."

*

"Who was on the phone?" Vanessa came out of the bathroom with a towel wrapped around her head.

"Dad called." Jeff lay on his belly on the floor, his brow furrowed with concentration as he arranged several plastic figurines in specific places. "He said he'll call again tomorrow. I told him I'm fine."

"Good. I'm going to go start supper." Vanessa stood in the hallway for a second and sagged against the wall. *They're fine, but I'm not.*

Staying in Nathan's home was a huge mistake. She'd been sleeping in the guest bedroom next to Jeff's, but even it carried Evie's stamp. No matter where she turned, Vanessa felt the lingering ghost of Nathan's wife—in the silk pansy arrangement on the bedside table, the Battenburg lace comforter and curtains, the kitchen's pink flowered dishes, floor, and wallpaper. Nathan couldn't bear to change Jeff's room, even though it looked woefully infantile. The first thing Vanessa did was to shut the door to Nathan's bedroom. A pair of portraits hung in there—one of Evie in her wedding gown, and another of her and Nathan.

Father, I went into this with the right intentions. Where did I go wrong?

She rewrapped her turban and dragged herself downstairs. Consuelo normally came in to do the housekeeping and laundry, but she had the flu. Vanessa tried to keep the house picked up as she went along, but between Jeff and Licorice, it wasn't a successful operation. She tucked his book bag against the couch, out of the way of traffic, and made a mental note that he still had to take a ruler to class tomorrow.

With Consuelo sick, Jeff didn't have anyone to go pick him up after school or watch him until Vanessa got off work. She juggled her schedule so Jamie was at the shop for the twenty minutes each afternoon that it took for her to zip over to the school and back. Jeff would do his homework in the back room, show it to Vanessa, then help her out with filling water bowls or playing with the animals. The makeshift arrangement actually worked out fairly smoothly.

Vanessa headed into the kitchen. Somewhere along the line, she'd gathered that Nathan's culinary skills encompassed the vital ability to open cans and microwave frozen foods. All week long, Jeff sat wide-eyed at the table as she put home-cooked meals in front of him. Tonight, she didn't have the energy. She opened a can of chili.

As it heated on the stove, the phone rang.

"I've got it!" Jeff shouted from the stairs. He rocketed across the living room and snagged the receiver. In a breathless voice, he said, "Hellowhoisthis?"

Vanessa bit her lip. Maybe they should talk about phone manners tonight at dinner.

"Van, it's for you."

She took the phone. "Hello?"

"Vanessa, this is Dave."

Dave. Dave from Guide Dogs. . . She mentally placed him and said, "Yes?"

"I've got a tough one for you. They're starting a new training session up at the facility on Monday. One of the dogs they were going to use just got held back. He got into a tussle with an unleashed boxer."

"He didn't get injured, did he?"

For all of their work, the hardest thing the puppy raisers had to deal with was unleashed dogs. They disrupted all but the most polished, obedient, mature puppies, and even then, it could be dicey.

"No, but we think he needs another couple of months of citizen training before we put him through the program. You've done a marvelous job with Amber, and I'd like to go ahead and slip her ahead into that position."

Vanessa drew in a quick breath.

"I know we had her slated to go in six weeks, Van." He spoke quietly, his words measured with understanding of the sacrifice he asked. Vanessa knew he'd raised a puppy and relinquished it—he knew firsthand how much it hurt. "It's hard to let them go, even with a target date."

She let out a long, choppy breath. "Is there any other candidate you could have go?"

"That last trip we all made to Disneyland is what made me think of you. Amber performed like a pro. She got on and off the Haunted Mansion and Pirates of the Caribbean like she'd been on them a million times. When that little girl came up and yanked on her tail, she showed exceptional tolerance too."

Vanessa remembered that trip. The puppy training club went on monthly outings to socialize and to expose the dogs to challenging situations. She'd posed Amber with characters for photos, sat on Main Street and watched the parade, and had been proud that Amber didn't bat an eye at the huge draft horses pulling a trolley.

In a small voice, she said, "So Amber passed the final, and

I didn't even know it was an exam."

"It wasn't meant to be, Van."

"I know. You've always been right up front with me. It's heartache talking. You know me." She laughed sadly. "Always talking before I think."

"I'll make the flight arrangements and get back to you. You've done a fine job, and someone is going to be lucky to have Amber as their guide dog."

"Thanks, Dave." She tearfully whispered, "Bye," and quickly hung up the phone.

"Van?" Jeff tugged on the hem of her sleeve. "What's wrong?"

"Everything."

❧

Nathan scowled at his cell phone. He'd accidentally left it on, and the charge was almost shot. He dialed home. "Van? Listen, my battery's almost gone. I won't be able to call tomorrow. How are things going?"

"Jeff's over at the Wilsons's for Caleb's pizza party."

"I forgot about that! I didn't get a present."

"I called Caleb's mom to get approval. He's now the proud owner of a second hamster."

"I owe you, big time. How about you?" Just then, his cell phone let out a pitiful beep. "Van? Van?"

He kicked a small stone, sending it flying into a metal trash can. The *ping* wasn't loud enough to tattle on his frustration, but Nathan hated having to wait to tell Vanessa his good news. Then again, he smiled to himself, it's the kind of news best given in person.

The next day, hundreds of tools rattled in the back of the truck. At one of the preplanning meetings, he'd assessed what folks were taking and deduced their team was grossly under supplied. His construction company had donated materials, and he'd packed a generator and all sorts of power and hand tools in his truck. He hit a pothole, and everything made another loud *clunk*. Nathan didn't care. Normally, he took pains to treat his tools well, but it didn't matter this time. He was going home, and he wanted to get there as soon as possible.

Kip understood. He'd helped Nathan pitch the tools in and shoved him toward the cab. "I'll take down the tent. You go on ahead and get home. You have someone waiting for you. . .and I don't mean Jeff."

Nathan had paused for an instant and given Kip a searching look.

"Vanessa is yours, Buddy." Kip lifted his blistered hands in a gesture of surrender. "I gave it a try, but I know when to quit. You're the right man for her. Now that you squared things away with God, there's nothing standing in the way. Go home. Make her a happy woman."

Nathan remembered Kip's words as he pulled onto his housing tract. Everything had fallen into place. Life had a sense of rightness. A neighbor was mowing his lawn, and a few kids were tossing a Frisbee. His son and the woman he loved were just a street away.

Instead of the welcome he expected, his reception was anything but delirious. Vanessa sat on the steps with her arm around Amber. Jeff sat on the other side of the retriever. All three of them looked glum.

Nathan had barely jammed his truck into "Park" when he bolted over to them. "What's wrong?"

Jeff popped up and gave him a hug. "Van has to give Amber back."

Vanessa's pretty blue eyes were red rimmed and puffy. If ever she needed comfort, now was the time. Nathan plopped down beside her and slid his arm around her shoulders. "When?"

"Tomorrow."

Even choking out that one word stretched her. Nathan could scarcely stand seeing her hurt. He tilted her head onto his shoulder and whispered into her soft, golden hair, "You can keep her if you really want to, can't you?"

Vanessa shook her head. "I gave my word. From the day I got her, I knew I'd have to let go."

"She's being honor'ble, Dad."

"Yes, Sport, she is." He wondered aloud, "How are you going to do it?"

She lifted her head and looked at him. Tears glistened in her eyes. "God loved His Son supremely—but when it came time for mankind to stop walking in darkness, to shed spiritual blindness, God sent his beloved Son to lead us to eternal freedom. It was an unspeakable sacrifice—but I'm eternally grateful for it."

He let her talk, not knowing where she was going, but willing to let her talk if it gave her any comfort.

"Each time I've given up a guide puppy I've trained, I've remembered God's sacrifice for my soul. I've had to trust Him to give me consolation. He's been faithful, and that's why I've always taken on another puppy. By giving up Amber, someone who lives in darkness can find liberty. It's nowhere near the scope of the Lord's sacrifice, but drawing that parallel helps me let go because God proved that by giving, we're set free. I'm just following His example."

Tears ran down her pale cheeks. Nathan wrapped her in his arms and held her as she cried. He'd spent the last months thinking she was so innocent in her faith, yet she'd been far wiser than he'd been. She'd let God come alongside her in her times of loss. Oh, to be sure, the loss of a guide puppy didn't in any way equate with his losing Evie, but the God who cared about the lilies of the field and counted every hair on a man's head certainly covered every concern with His love.

Vanessa sniffled and pushed away.

"Van, we need to talk." He wanted to tell her his good news, to maybe shed some light in the midst of her sadness.

"No." She dipped her head. "I need time alone with Amber. I really need to go."

"Can't you stay just a little while? Maybe I could take a quick shower, and we could go out for supper."

"No."

"I'll drive you home. You shouldn't be driving right now."

"I need to drive. It'll help me clear my head." She flipped a swath of hair behind her shoulder and stood. Pasting on a smile that was anything but genuine, she said, "Jeff is a terrific kid. You can be proud of him."

"I'll help you put your stuff in the car."

She pulled her key ring from the pocket of her jeans. "Jeff already helped me. I need to go. G'bye."

He fought the urge to snatch her back, to hold her and let her pour out every last tear. She wanted to spend this last night alone with Amber, and she deserved that. Nathan stood on the porch and watched her drive off. If he had his way, she wouldn't be doing that again.

❧

Amber sensed something was wrong. She gently nosed Vanessa. That action opened the floodgates. Vanessa sat on the floor by her bed, wrapped her arms around her puppy, buried her face in her fur, and wept. Everything in her life felt like it was falling apart. She had no one to blame but herself.

She'd chosen to take on this puppy. All along, she'd known the time would come to give her up. What kind of fool was she to keep setting herself up for this kind of parting?

And then there was Nathan. The tears flowed even faster,

wetting Amber's soft coat. Mom and Dad and Val and even Kip had warned her. They'd each come to her and discussed their concerns. *Oh, but did I listen? No.*

In the week that she'd cared for Jeff, she'd come to realize how much she adored him. The feeling was obviously mutual. He was a great kid. Cute. Smart. Tenderhearted, grubby faced, and ultimately lovable.

The first few nights, she'd looked forward to a cell phone call from Nathan. Then she'd grown to dread them. As she stayed in his home, the truth became undeniable. What started out as an innocent business arrangement had ensnared her, and she couldn't let the relationship continue.

Vanessa had to face the heart-wrenching fact that she'd unwisely let her heart get ahead of her spiritual welfare. A huge ball formed in her throat.

God, I've been so foolish, so arrogant. All along, I thought I was in control of my feelings. Ever since I accepted You, I knew I was meant to fall in love with a man who wanted to serve You as much as I did. In my dreams, we were going to have a marriage based on You as our foundation.

I didn't listen. Mom and Dad came to me. Val tried to talk sense into me, and Kip even confronted me. Instead of listening to wise counsel, I charged ahead. I really thought I was doing the right thing. I wore my faith as a shield and thought it would serve as a barrier against any heartbreak. How wrong I've been!

I love him, God. I do. I hate to admit it to myself and to confess it to You. How did I come to this point? In the past, I'd been so positive about setting my affections on a man who was on fire for Your kingdom. Nathan is burned out, yet I want him.

I know I have to make a choice. Nothing can come between me and You. Abraham faced having to choose, and he was willing to sacrifice Isaac. You gave Your Son. Nathan professes to still be Your child, but he isn't walking with You. What kind of home

*would we have if the foundation isn't built on Your will and holy
Word? If my husband isn't following You, how can he lead me?
What about any children we'd have? I know it's wrong. Father, I
know it's so very wrong.*

*But in my heart, I long for Nathan to be restored to You. His
bitterness has faded into. . .emotionless acceptance. It's progress,
but it isn't enough. I have faith You can reclaim him. Until he
comes to that point, I see how I cannot let the love I feel flourish. I
don't know how to stop it. I've never understood how Abraham
could put his son on the altar. Can't you work a miracle for me,
just as you did for him?*

*Give me strength to cling to You and let go of Nathan. Help me
make the right choices. Give me the courage to let go.*

No grand or glorious thing happened. She didn't feel a
blanket of peace descend. If anything, her prayer only served
to sharpen her awareness of just where she stood. Tears
burned behind her eyelids, and a deep ache radiated behind
her breastbone.

She'd hoped for a fleeting moment that Nathan would say
something when she spoke about giving Amber away, but
he'd been silent.

Even if he did reestablish a firm relationship with the Lord,
Nathan still loved Evie. His heart belonged to the woman
who had borne his child. So did his home—their home, the
charming little saltbox Evie rescued on their honeymoon and
Nathan lovingly reconstructed for her. Every single room still
looked as she'd decorated it. Her pictures hung on walls and
sat in frames on tables. All of the patience in the world
wouldn't erase his memories, and Vanessa came to the conclusion she simply couldn't shadowbox the rest of her life with
a memory.

Amber. Strike one. Nathan's soul. Strike two. Nathan's
heart. Strike three.

Vanessa tipped her head back and stared at the ceiling. The light fixture wavered and formed a halo because of her tears. "God, I've struck out. I can't do this on my own. What more do You want from me?"

twenty

"Vanessa, let me drive you and Amber to the airport."

"Thanks, Nathan. It's nice of you to offer, but I have to do this myself."

"Honey—"

"I need to go. Bye." She hung up. Putting the bright green jacket on Amber was hard. It was yet another "last time" thing she was doing today. "You're a big girl now. You'll go to doggy college and wear a blue jacket."

Secretly, there was that selfish wish that Amber would go and "flunk out." Then, she could come back forever. . . . Vanessa clenched her eyes shut to keep from crying. *God, I really don't want to be that kind of person. Make me bigger than my selfish desires.*

Amber usually traveled in passenger compartments. She'd been on a plane twice and on a boat, busses, trains, even a hay wagon. Today was different. At the airport, Vanessa stayed with her until the very last moment, gave her a hug and kiss, and put her in a dog crate. She wept as they took Amber off to the plane, cried all of the way home, and flung herself across her bed. She lay at the very edge, her fingertips brushing the edge of Amber's bed. It was as empty as her aching heart.

❧

Nathan had tried to contact Vanessa a half-dozen times in the last twenty-four hours, and she'd given him every version of a polite brush-off he'd ever seen. He wasn't going to put up with it any longer.

Nathan chuckled under his breath. Vanessa, impulsive in so many ways, managed to model patience. Today, he was the impulsive one, and he had no patience left. He strode to her door with resolve, gave it three solid raps, and jangled the keys in his pocket as he waited for her to answer. She didn't come, so he banged on the door a few more times. Still no response.

Unwilling to give up, he hiked around the corner of her place and drummed his fingers on her bedroom window. When he'd helped move Val out, he'd had a conniption that they were on a ground floor with no security. He'd come back and put in a security window. Now, he wished he hadn't.

One side of the curtain inched back. "Whaddo you want?"

"Doing that well, huh?"

The curtains opened wider, revealing a very sleepy woman bundled in a robe the color of shamrocks. Nathan thought she looked as if someone tackled her and wrapped her up in AstroTurf. She'd never looked better to him. She scrubbed her face with her palm, then swept her wild hair back behind her left ear. "Do you have any idea what time it is?"

"Time to talk. Get dressed."

"Nathan, go home."

"No can do. Hurry up."

She turned to the side and wheeled back around. Her eyes were huge. "It's five-fifteen. Are you crazy? Who's watching Jeff?"

"Val is. I know what time it is, and we'll be late if you don't get a move on."

"The only place I'm going is back to bed." The curtains swished shut.

Nathan chuckled. He didn't doubt for a minute she'd be headed right back to bed, but he wasn't about to let her do it. He drummed his fingers on the window.

"Go away!" came the muffled shout.

A set of sprinklers started on the far side of the lawn. *I'm going to get soaked. May as well be a fool for love.* . . . He cleared his throat and began to sing. "It's rain-ing, it's pour-ing, the old man is—"

The curtains didn't open. Vanessa popped up from beneath them like a crazed jack-in-the-box and flipped the safety latch on the window. Her cheeks glowed scarlet. As she opened the double-thick, shatterproof pane, she hissed hotly, "If you had any sense at all, you'd just leave." She drew in a breath and added, "Can't you see the sprinklers are coming on?"

"Why do you think I'm singing this song?"

"I have no idea. I didn't recognize it as music. The first time you sang it with Jeff was cute, but this is irri—"

"Jeans and a sweatshirt, Van. Put 'em on and meet me at the front door." He glanced down at his wristwatch. "You have ten minutes."

"You have ten seconds to go away before I call the police. You're disturbing my peace!"

"Nine minutes."

She huffed and shut the window. He heard her mattress squeak.

Four minutes later, he used his cell phone and called her. "Five minutes, and I have chocolate."

❧

He'd given her five minutes. . .like he had any right to make any dictates to her. Still, he had her so tied in knots, she wasn't going to get back to sleep, anyway. Vanessa clambered out of bed and headed toward her closet. He'd specified jeans and a sweatshirt, but she wasn't going anywhere. Not at this hour. Not with him. She yanked on jeans, but her sweatshirts were in the bottom drawer over where Amber's empty bed lay. She couldn't go over there right now. Not a chance. She'd start crying all over again. Instead, Vanessa rummaged through her closet and pulled out a T-shirt that was as blue as she felt.

In her haste, she broke her shoelace. "Ohh!" She flung that shoe across the room and listened to the satisfying *thump* it made as it hit the floor right next to her shoe rack. Even in her frustration, at least she managed to keep her aim true. She scowled at her feet and hobbled over to that shoe rack. "Oh, forget it." She stopped looking and twist-stepped into big, rainbow-striped, fuzzy slippers.

Nathan Adams was about to get a piece of her mind. "Let's go." As soon as she said the command for Amber, she realized for the millionth time that Amber was gone. All of those things she said and did as a puppy trainer were empty gestures and phrases now—and painful reminders of the loss she'd sustained. A fresh wave of grief washed over her.

Nathan knocked at the front door.

Vanessa marched over, jerked open the front door, and gave him a belligerent look. How dare he show up at this ridiculous hour at all, let alone looking like that? Freshly shaven, lounging against her door frame, he could have just stepped from a magazine ad.

"Good morning, Sweetheart."

"Give me the chocolates, and you might not get hurt."

"They're in the car." He grabbed hold of her wrist and yanked.

Vanessa struggled to free herself. "What in the world are you doing?"

"Kidnapping you."

"You're nuts. I don't want to go anywhere or do anything. Just leave me alone."

He tilted his head to the side, and his dark brown eyes shone with compassion. "Hiding out won't take away the pain, Honey."

"Neither will running all over the place."

"True, but I have special plans. You'll have to trust me." He glanced down and shook his head. "I've got an extra sweatshirt in the car, but those slippers won't do."

"Just what is wrong with my slippers?" She folded her arms across her chest and tapped her toe.

"They'll get wet when you walk across the lawn."

"I'm not walking across the lawn!"

Nathan gave her a don't-be-difficult look. All of a sudden, he ducked, rammed his shoulder into her middle, and wrapped his arm around the backs of her legs. When he straightened up, she dangled over his shoulder like a rag doll. She turned her head to the side, saw him snatch her key ring from the hall table, then dizzily watched as he pulled the door shut and locked it.

She tried to stay calm. "What are you doing?"

"We've already discussed that. I'm kidnapping you and your goofy slippers. I'm even making sure they don't get wet."

A considerate kidnapper. She'd chalk this all up as another one of her wild nightmares, but blood rushed to her head. It pulsed and made her ears ring, proving she really was awake and Nathan truly had gone 'round the bend. "Let me get this straight. Valene is with Jeff and knows you're doing this?"

"Yup. So do your parents."

"Now I've heard everything."

"Almost. I've arranged for Jamie and your mom to mind the shop today."

"Great." She tried to catch her breath. It wasn't exactly an easy thing to do in this position. "I'm getting abducted by approval."

Nathan's shoulder shook as he chortled, and the action made her bounce. *It would serve him right if I threw up all over his legs. He's having far too much fun, and I don't want to play this game.*

"Really, Nathan, take me back. I'm lousy company right now."

"I'll take you however you come." He stopped, opened the car door, and lowered her inside with surprising care instead of dumping her like a sack of cement. He slammed her door shut, zipped around the car, and slid into the driver's seat.

Just then, Vanessa caught sight of herself in the visor's mirror and let out a breathless shriek. "Okay, the joke's over. I'm going back inside."

He started the car and put it into motion before she could open her door. "Buckle up, and the chocolate is in the glove compartment."

"I haven't brushed my hair. I don't have any makeup on, and I'm wearing slippers!"

"Yeah, so?" He shifted and pulled a black comb from his pocket. "Borrow this. Eat the chocolate."

She made a rude huff as she accepted the comb. The man needed to get his head examined if he thought this was going to mollify her.

"You're a natural beauty, Sweetheart. You don't need a bunch of stuff all over your pretty face, and as for your slippers. . ." He let go of the steering wheel momentarily and lifted his palms in an "oh well" gesture.

Vanessa pulled the comb through her tangles and gave him a disgruntled look. Leave it to him to give her a compliment on a morning like this. Clueless. The man was utterly clueless. Good thing too. It meant she could stay mad at him about this escapade and use it as an excuse to distance herself and cool the relationship.

"So ask me about what I found in Mexico."

"Obviously you lost your wits."

"This is important, Van."

"Sure it is," she said flippantly. She tossed his comb onto the dashboard and rooted around in the glove compartment for the chocolate. Nothing. She unbuckled her seat belt and twisted around.

"You're not listening to me."

Desperation had her rummaging through the stuff he had stored in the backseat. She didn't want to face him right now. "You promised me chocolate."

Nathan's baritone filled the car:

" 'When peace like a river attendeth my way,
When sorrows like sea billows roll,
Whatever my lot, Thou hast taught me to say,
It is well, it is well, with my soul.' "

Vanessa twisted around and stared at him. She clamped her hand around his arm and squeezed. "What?"

He gave her a soul-stirring smile. "I found my way back. My relationship with Christ is on track again."

"Oh, praise God!"

"The hurt and anger are gone, Van. I realized what a fool I was for blaming God for robbing me of my wife. Evie was His child, and He called her home. For a time, I was blessed to have her to love. I've mourned for her, and I'll always miss her, but now I can be at peace, knowing she's whole and healthy in heaven."

Vanessa took a deep breath. She didn't want to hear about Evie. Even the mere mention of her name was like a dagger through her heart, but how selfish was that? Nathan was freed of his shackles, and that was what was important. He'd begun to heal spiritually.

"Wow. Answered prayer."

"I know you were faithful to pray for me, Van." He gave her a piercing look, then trained his gaze back on the road. "I managed to push away everyone else, but you were different.

You didn't push back or walk away. You've stuck around and let God work in His own way."

"So tell me about how God finally got through to you!"

"It's been so subtle—gradual, you know? At first, I couldn't stand anything having to do with worshiping Him. All of the essentials for a strong walk stopped cold. But God's used you to patiently reintroduce them to me: associating with believers, prayer, attending church." He hitched his shoulder. "The final step was down in Mexico. Kip got me to start reading God's Word again."

"Kip's a great friend, Nathan."

"Yeah, he is—to me. What about you?"

Father, how do I respond to this? The biggest hurdle is behind us—Nathan is Yours. With time, can he let go of Evie and learn to love me? Do I play it safe and tell him Kip is just a friend, or do I focus on the relationship that may or may not ever blossom between me and this man?

Vanessa took a deep breath and looked Nathan in the eye. "I hope I'm a great friend to you too."

His rich, deep laughter filled the cab. Vanessa had the feeling she'd mistakenly answered Nathan's question the wrong way, but nothing mattered this morning.

"I finally realized the truth—I'd been longing for what was right in front of me all of those years. I was like a blind man, wandering around in darkness. I let anger and grief come between me and God instead of letting Him be my strength and solace at the darkest time in my life. Now I've come back to the Light. God's restored my spirit—just as he did for David in the Psalms."

"I'm so happy for you, Nathan."

"It's the craziest thing. I kept thinking the emptiness and loneliness were because I was a widower. I'm still a widower, but I can see that when grief should have started to wane, I stayed so empty because I'd shut down spiritually. You have no idea how free I feel."

His news started to fully sink in. He hadn't just made a decision with his mind—his heart and soul were behind it. The joy flowing from him touched her deeply.

"You once said God was bigger than my anger," Nathan continued. "I had plenty of people tell me I was a sinner for that; you were patient with me and let God chip away at my hardened heart. He is bigger than anything that I am or feel or do. But the other thing is, He doesn't expect me to pretend—He already knows how I feel, so I can live honestly before Him."

Vanessa nodded.

"I'm not trapped in the past anymore, Vanessa."

"The chains are broken. I'm glad for you."

He'd zipped down the freeway and turned onto a winding dirt road. Now he made a sharp hairpin and another wild jog to one side. A hot-air balloon came into sight.

"Oh, look!"

Nathan parked the truck and turned to her. "I wanted to celebrate with you in a special way. Let's go."

Still stunned by everything he'd said, Vanessa got out of the car when he opened her door. She watched him yank a paint-splattered, maroon sweatshirt from the back of his truck and gladly accepted it. Once she pulled it over her head, he slipped his strong hand along the back of her neck and freed her hair. The sudden warmth felt good in the nippy morning air, but she wasn't sure whether it was from the sweatshirt, his good news, or his touch.

"Come on." He took her hand and led her all of one step, then stopped. He looked down at her slippers and shook his head. "Upsy-daisy."

Vanessa let out a surprised squeal as he scooped her into his arms.

Nathan carried her toward the balloon and stopped briefly to speak with one of the men who seemed to be directing the busy ground crew. Seemingly satisfied, Nathan gave her a squeeze and carried her to the basket.

"Ready to go?" the operator inside the basket shouted above the din.

Nathan raised a brow as he looked at her. She nodded enthusiastically, so he lifted her into the basket, then climbed in beside her. He stood close in the tight quarters and bumped a picnic basket with his knee. He pointed down, then put his mouth by her ear and half-shouted, "Once we get underway, you can have some coffee. I ordered breakfast for us."

"Breakfast on thin air? How fun!"

The basket shifted a bit beneath their feet. Vanessa grabbed one of the lines. Nathan grabbed her. She didn't mind one bit.

Filled with hot air, the balloon barely started to rise. "Away we go!" someone said from behind her. The noise from the burners ripped through the air and made any conversation virtually impossible. The ground seemed to fall away and their balloon continued to rise. The movement felt smooth, but the height change seemed almost dizzying. Soon Nathan's car resembled one of Jeff's toys. A stand of trees looked like frilled toothpicks. As they reached cruising altitude, the noise from the burners diminished.

"Isn't this outta sight?" Nathan's arm around her waist tightened.

"Amazing! I've always wanted to ride in one of these!" She let go of one of the lines and reached out. "I almost feel like I can touch the clouds from here."

Nathan turned her and held her close. His warmth and strength felt marvelous. Slowly, one of his hands slid up her back to her nape. He spread his fingers out and speared them through her hair, forcing her to face him.

Vanessa didn't want to look at him. If she did, he'd be able to read her like a book and know exactly how she felt about him. She tried to turn her head to the side. "Look at the horizon. We're going right toward the sunrise!"

"I don't need to look out there to see today or tomorrow." He exerted gentle pressure and had her staring up at him.

Vanessa could scarcely catch her breath.

"I'm already walking on clouds, Van, and when I look at you, I see all of the bright days ahead."

He caught her gasp with a toe-curling kiss. When he lifted his head, he smiled. "I've been wanting to do that for awhile."

"Oh, my."

"I've already gone to your dad and mom. We have their blessing."

"Their blessing," she echoed, hoping she understood his meaning but afraid she was letting her wishes run wild.

"I know this is our first date, but I'm going to court you for a lifetime. I can't wait, though." Nathan's arm cinched tighter around her waist. He dipped his head and nuzzled her ear. "Marry me, Vanessa."

"Was that a request or a command?"

"It's a requirement." He pulled away a little and pressed his forehead to hers. "Live with me and love with me and laugh with me. God fills my soul, but you fill my heart."

There under a zigzag rainbow fabric canopy, soaring toward a sunny day, Vanessa didn't have to give more than a second's consideration to his proposal. "Yes, Nathan. I'd love to be your wife."

"Seal it with a kiss," he said in a husky tone.

After a kiss that promised happily-ever-afters, he cuddled closer. "Happy?"

She nodded, stood on the tiptoes of her slippers, and wrapped her arms around his neck. "I never want to touch down. I've been going crazy, loving a man who was so blind."

He looked deeply into her eyes. "Sweetheart, I can see forever from here."

epilogue

Vanessa sat in the bride's room, brushed on a touch of mascara, and winked at Della. "I have a feeling you like these clothes better than our baseball uniforms."

Della fluffed her hair. "Don't you just know it? You taught me how to bat and how to snag a ball. Think you can teach me how to catch a husband?"

"We'll have to see if Nathan invited any good prospects. I'll have him introduce you and Valene to them at the reception."

Valene groaned.

Vanessa gave her twin a saucy smile in the mirror. "Guess what I just figured out?"

"What?" Valene adjusted the skirt of her smoky blue maid-of-honor dress until it hung with sheer grace.

Her twin had been fussing all morning, and Vanessa suspected it was because she hated to be on stage at all. Even being a maid of honor was more spotlight than she'd prefer to handle, but she filled the role because sisterly love trumped shyness. Vanessa decided to tease her to help lighten her anxiety.

"When we walk down the aisle, it's the last time in my life I'm going to be the last one. Alphabetically, I've always been dead last."

Della snorted. "What did you expect? With a last name like Zobel, you were sunk."

"No kidding," Val agreed.

"Yeah, but you still came before me," Vanessa said to her sister. "Val, then Van. My married name will be Adams." She stood and twirled about in her rustling satin slips. "And the last shall come first. . . ."

Mom made a worried sound and started to take the bridal gown off of the hanger. "If you don't get into this gown, you're not going to be first or last. You'll be an old maid."

"Are you kidding? Nathan would marry me if I walked out there in my ugly orange baseball uniform. He proposed to me in my rainbow slippers."

Della gave her a silly look. "Let me get this straight. He was wearing your slippers?"

"And you all think I'm daffy? Of course he wasn't. Have you seen the size of his feet? I was wearing them when he kidnapped me. It was so romantic."

Val held part of the bridal gown, and Della took hold of another section. "Come on. Let's get this woman into her gown before she gets so besotted with those stupid slippers, she wants to get married in them." They lifted the gown so Vanessa could slip into it.

As Val started to do up the zipper of the dreams-come-true satin-and-lace bridal gown, Vanessa worried aloud, "You all have everything you need, right? Jeff will stay with Val for the next few days, then he'll go stay with Mom and Dad. Mom, you and Dad will stop by Nathan's and get Lick tonight? He'll tear up Val's condo. He needs your big backyard to romp in."

"Stop worrying," Val chided. "You're chewing off your lipstick."

"Girlfriend, you need to get your head examined." Della shook her finger at Van. "You're going off on a romantic honeymoon to Ireland and Scotland, and you're fretting about a dumb dog?"

"That dog and a silly goldfish are what brought them together," Valene said loyally.

"Yes." Vanessa dipped down so her mother could help her pin on an airy veil. She left the blusher veil back out of the way for the present. "And so did the grace and mercy of God."

Someone tapped on the door. Della opened it.

Dad stuck his head into the room. "We're ready."

Jeff nudged past him and stared up at Vanessa. His little mouth dropped open. He blinked, then said in an awed tone, "You look like a fairy princess."

"Yes, Kitten, you do." Her father's voice sounded choked.

Jeff walked all the way around her and asked, "Do I get to call you 'Mom' now?"

"That would make me so happy!"

"Okay, Mom. Daddy said he wanted you to hurry up. He said he's waited long enough for his sweetheart. Did you know that's what he called you?"

"Yes." She smiled at the way Jeff wrinkled his nose. At the rehearsal the day before, Nathan had been eager to sweep her into a theatrical dip and give her a heart-stopping kiss. Jeff ended it all with a loud, "Eww, yuck!" Nathan later borrowed her strawberry lip gloss and let Jeff take a whiff. After that, Jeff decided his dad hadn't gone crazy, after all. His favorite bubble gum smelled like that. Nathan then had extracted a pledge from his "honor'ble" son that he wouldn't make any noises during the real wedding ceremony.

They all went to the narthex. Mom gave Vanessa one last kiss and allowed Kip to seat her before he took his place as best man. The music started, and Jeff carried a satin pillow with the rings tied to it. He stopped partway down the aisle to scratch his knee, then continued on with all the decorum of an English butler.

Della stepped off, and Val turned to Vanessa. She didn't say a word. She didn't need to. They'd always been able to communicate at moments like this with just a look. She nodded, smiled, and headed down the aisle.

"Kitten, he's a good man, a godly man. I had some real doubts awhile back, but I know he's the man I prayed for God to bring to you."

"Thank you, Daddy." She gave him a kiss, accepted his fumbling help to pull down her blusher veil, and took his arm.

Vanessa walked down the aisle with every assurance that waiting for this moment was worth every prayer she'd ever whispered. When she could see Nathan at the front of the church, she knew she'd never known a more handsome man. Love and happiness shone in his eyes. Daddy gave her away, and she stood beside Nathan, then knelt at the altar.

They'd consulted and counseled with Pastor MacIntosh, and now he began to read the Scripture they'd requested for their wedding. It was from 1 Corinthians:

"Love is patient. . . ."

A Letter To Our Readers

Dear Reader:

In order that we might better contribute to your reading enjoyment, we would appreciate your taking a few minutes to respond to the following questions. We welcome your comments and read each form and letter we receive. When completed, please return to the following:

Fiction Editor
Heartsong Presents
PO Box 719
Uhrichsville, Ohio 44683

1. Did you enjoy reading *Love Is Patient* by Cathy Marie Hake?
❑ Very much! I would like to see more books by this author!
❑ Moderately. I would have enjoyed it more if

_____

_____

_____

2. Are you a member of **Heartsong Presents**? ❑ Yes ❑ No
If no, where did you purchase this book? _____

_____

3. How would you rate, on a scale from 1 (poor) to 5 (superior), the cover design? _____

4. On a scale from 1 (poor) to 10 (superior), please rate the following elements.

____ Heroine	____ Plot
____ Hero	____ Inspirational theme
____ Setting	____ Secondary characters

5. These characters were special because? _____
_____
_____

6. How has this book inspired your life? _____
_____
_____

7. What settings would you like to see covered in future
   Heartsong Presents books? _____
_____
_____

8. What are some inspirational themes you would like to see
   treated in future books? _____
_____
_____

9. Would you be interested in reading other **Heartsong
   Presents** titles? ❏ Yes   ❏ No

10. Please check your age range:
   ❏ Under 18   ❏ 18-24
   ❏ 25-34   ❏ 35-45
   ❏ 46-55   ❏ Over 55

Name _____
Occupation _____
Address _____
City_____ State_____ Zip_____

VANCOUVER

What's the best thing about living in a beautiful modern city— being surrounded by buildings, people, and activity? Or just getting away from it all? Meet four women who hold differing views of life in Canada's jeweled city.

Laugh and cry with these resourceful Canadian women and watch how faith and love uphold them on drifting currents of life.

Contemporary, paperback, 480 pages, 5 $^3/_{16}$" x 8"

❤ ❤ ❤ ❤ ❤ ❤ ❤ ❤ ❤ ❤ ❤ ❤ ❤ ❤ ❤

❤ ❤ ❤ ❤ ❤ ❤ ❤ ❤ ❤ ❤ ❤ ❤ ❤ ❤ ❤

Heartsong

Any 12 Heartsong Presents titles for only $30.00*

CONTEMPORARY ROMANCE IS CHEAPER BY THE DOZEN!

Buy any assortment of twelve *Heartsong Presents* titles and save 25% off of the already discounted price of $3.25 each!

*plus $2.00 shipping and handling per order and sales tax where applicable.

HEARTSONG PRESENTS TITLES AVAILABLE NOW:

(If ordering from this page, please remember to include it with the order form.)